文法是英文學習不可或缺的一環，

有了文法觀念才能**串連單字**、**片語**，進而**組成句子**，

現在，跟著薄冰老師

用最淺顯、清楚、易懂的方式和大量例句學英文文法

想要從頭開始，就選：

五億人重新開始的第一本英文文法書！

捷徑文化
Royal Road Publishing Group

　　在2011年和2012年，我陸續為薄冰老師的三本文法書撰寫過推薦序與導讀，依序是：《五億人都在看的英文文法書》、《五億人的第一本國中英文文法書》、《五億人的第一本高中英文文法書》。這三本書的讀者群分別為大專生、社會人士（或進階讀者）、國中生、高中生。上市以來，這一系列文法著作廣受台灣讀者歡迎。

　　很高興，捷徑出版社再度推出薄冰老師的另一續作——《五億人重新開始的第一本英文文法書》。簡要的說，這本最新著作就是一本英文初階文法，適合的讀者是英文初學者，以及有心重新學習英文的各階層人士。

　　但初階文法並不是把進階文法的內容濃縮刪節即可。從學習的角度來看，初階文法的編排難度有時更甚於進階文法，因為初階文法的讀者是初學者，如何使初學者輕鬆跨進英文的領域，如何使初學者建立學習英文的信心，這是一本初階文法書該努力達成的目標。

　　薄冰老師的《五億人重新開始的第一本英文文法書》很接近我心中理想的初階文法書。在這本書中，我至少看到下列的優點：

一、內容簡單扼要，只談最重要的文法概念。文法的解說以通則為主，很少談到例外的部份。但如有重要的觀念需釐清，也有「注

意」專欄以明顯的排版設計提醒讀者。

二、內容有趣易學，避免過度強調文法術語，對初學者或文法底子不
　　好的人來說，很容易入門。

三、文法術語的定義清晰明瞭，有些定義能另闢蹊徑，對讀者有極大
　　幫助。

四、舉例與現實生活連結，避免抽象高論。

五、提供適量的練習題，題型豐富也有鑑別度，能夠協助讀者立即檢
　　驗學習成果。

六、難易適中，整體內容足以啟發讀者，也能夠建立讀者的信心。

　　這是一本好用、容易上手的初階文法書。有興趣的讀者不妨翻閱
一下本書Unit 1的名詞篇，你就能立刻感受到，原來透過薄冰老師的
說明，理解個體名詞、集體名詞、物質名詞、抽象名詞等概念一點都
不難。

2012年12月於台北文山

Recommended

常常有人問我，怎麼樣才能把英文學好（或怎麼樣才能讓孩子學好英文）？依我多年英語教學的經驗來說，我的建議是：

一、找幾本字彙難易度適中、內容有趣的改編版小說，培養不查單字的閱讀方式（閱讀時可先將難字標記，讀完全書或一個章節之後再回頭查單字）。

二、先從收聽初階的英語雜誌著手，持續訓練聽力（初學者不用急著聽ICRT或看CNN，因為內容太難太快，容易打擊信心）。

三、跟讀（即模仿）初階程度的雜誌解說內容，或美國之音的慢速英文，可以訓練口說。

（註：美國之音VOA：Voice of America是美國政府設立的知名廣播電台與電視台。播出的內容包括新聞時事、專題節目、英語教學節目、美國流行音樂⋯⋯等，是知名的國際廣播之一。）

此外，還應該準備一本英文文法書。文法能夠幫助學習者理解單字、詞組、句子的結構，是一把通往英文精熟的鑰匙。良好的文法基礎有助於閱讀與聽力的理解；良好的文法基礎更是英文寫作的先備條件。

對於英文初學者以及重拾英文興趣的讀者而言，薄冰老師的《五億人重新開始的第一本英文文法書》是值得推薦的文法入門書。這本書最大的優點就是文法術語的解說自成一格，非常清晰易懂。此外，書中設計了各種練習題，難易適中，可供讀者立即演練，立即驗收。

　　對於英文學習者而言，能夠持續吸引你的注意，讓你充滿信心、興趣盎然地讀下去的書，才是最適合的書。我認為讀者看過薄冰的《五億人重新開始的第一本英文文法書》後，應該會贊同我的看法。

2012年12月於台北

　　近年來，英語學習的熱度仍不斷攀升，而學習英語的年齡層也呈現兩極化現象：

一、學習的起始年齡層逐年下降，不僅許多孩子從小學即開始學習英語，甚至很多家長砸大錢讓孩子從幼稚園就開始讀雙語學校，目的就是希望孩子要「贏在起跑點」！

二、有越來越多的人，不分年紀、不分職業領域，都很想好好把英文從頭學好。可能是一般上班族希望再充實自己，可能是家庭主婦也想讓自己仍能繼續求知學習，甚至是事業有成的主管階級將語言能力視為讓自己更有領導力的首要模範。

　　然而，因應這龐大的學習需求，市面上的英語學習讀物、書籍雖然琳琅滿目，但是真正要找一本符合當前各種學習者：必須打好基礎的初學者、視英語學習為孩子的「成才之道」、「成功之道」的家長、繁忙上班族、底子不好的二度學習者，真正適合的英文文法書卻少之又少。

　　在本書之前，我已與捷徑文化出版社合作推出了《五億人都在看的英文文法書》、《五億人的第一本國中英文文法書》、《五億人的第一本高中英文文法書》，前幾本主要都針對不同的學習階段來發想。但這一次，我和捷徑文

化總編輯都希望能推出一本適用於更多人、造福更多學習需求，尤其是需要從基礎學好，建立英文學習信心的初學者，以及很想從頭把英文學好、卻苦無一本真正能循序漸進的書帶領他一步步從頭學起的人。於是這本《五億人重新開始的第一本英文文法書》因而誕生。

這本書，我與許多熟悉英語教學的專家共同研討、編寫而成，在許多文法觀念的建構上，我們都花費了許多心思，考慮到以最簡明、白話的解釋，讓讀者明瞭；也以大量例句和多樣的練習題，讓大家一步一步地跟學、跟著做。不僅要除去一般大眾對於文法書嚴肅的刻板印象，更要讓初學、以及二度學習的您們，相信英文是不可怕的，只要選對教材、循序漸進、踏實地多加演練，定能重拾學習信心，成效也會一天天逐漸彰顯。

筆者真誠希望此書的出版，能為廣大英語學習的讀者助一臂之力，取得事半功倍的功用。

薄冰

2012 於北京

目錄 Contents

Unit 1. 名詞

Unit 2. 冠詞

Unit 3. 代名詞

Unit 4. 形容詞

Unit 5. 副詞

Unit 6. 數量詞

Unit 7. 介系詞

Unit 11. 動詞的時態

Unit 12. 直述句

Unit 13. 疑問句

Unit 14. 祈使句

Unit 15. 感嘆句

Unit 16. There be 句型

Unit 1.
名詞

Unit 1. 名詞

1. 讓我們來認識名詞

名詞是什麼呢？舉凡表示人、動物、地點、物品還有抽象概念，例如：戰爭、和平之類的詞，都屬於名詞。

人	
Jerry	傑瑞
artist	畫家
singer	歌手
teacher	老師
girl	女孩
boy	男孩

動物	
dog	狗
lion	獅子
zebra	斑馬
panda	熊貓
shark	鯊魚
dolphin	海豚

地點	
airport	機場
park	公園
school	學校
library	圖書館
beach	海灘
hotel	飯店

物品	
pencil	鉛筆
eraser	橡皮擦
table	桌子
sofa	沙發
car	汽車
airplane	飛機

抽象概念	
war	戰爭
peace	和平
honesty	誠實
courage	勇氣
anger	憤怒
wish	願望

2. 專有名詞和普通名詞

根據名詞的意義，我們可以將它分為專有名詞和普通名詞。

1. 專有名詞

表示特定的人或事物名稱的詞就叫做專有名詞。

人名	
Peter	彼得
Newton	牛頓
Snow White	白雪公主
Mr. Green	格林先生
Santa Claus	聖誕老人

星期、月份、節日	
Sunday	星期天
May	五月
Christmas	耶誕節
the Spring Festival	春節

建築、街道	
the Great Wall	長城
the Eiffel Tower	艾菲爾鐵塔
the Louvre Palace	羅浮宮
Downing Street	唐寧街
the Fifth Avenue	第五大道

國家、城市	
China	中國
Britain	英國
Beijing	北京
Paris	巴黎
Venice	威尼斯

要注意喔！

1. 專有名詞的第一個字母一定要大寫。
2. 你的名字還有你朋友的名字，都是屬於專有名詞，別忘了喔！

2. 普通名詞

　　普通名詞，其實就是專有名詞的相反。只要是不屬於特定的人、事、物名稱的詞，就叫做普通名詞。普通名詞又可分為：個體名詞、集體名詞、物質名詞、抽象名詞。聽起來好像很困難，其實一點也不會！讓我們一起看看底下的範例吧！

個體名詞	
cup	杯子
scarf	圍巾
guitar	吉他
taxi	計程車

集體名詞	
class	班級
family	家庭
people	人民
army	軍隊

物質名詞	
milk	牛奶
air	空氣
wood	木頭
sand	沙子

抽象名詞	
work	工作
health	健康
trust	信任
interest	興趣

個體名詞：指的是一個一個的東西，簡單來説，就是你用手，就可以「拿起來」，或者是「碰到」的東西，像是杯子、圍巾、吉他，就屬於「個體名詞」。

集體名詞：説的是一種「集合」的概念，例如一群人聚在一起，在教室上課，我們就可以稱為「班級」；家裡面有爸爸、媽媽、妹妹，還有你，這樣四個人聚在一起的地方，就是我們説的「家」。

物質名詞：物質名詞指的是我們統稱一樣東西的名稱，例如：牛奶、空氣、木頭、沙子。你可能會覺得很奇怪，咦？那這樣「物質名詞」跟「個體名詞」又有什麼不同呢？一般來説，物質名詞，是無法指稱的詞。例

如：沙子，你不會説「這個沙子」和「那個沙子」。但是説到個體名詞時，我們可以説：「這個杯子」、「那個杯子」，「你的杯子」、「我的杯子」。

抽象名詞：抽象名詞，就是我們無法「計算」跟「度量」的東西或事情，通常是抽象的概念，例如健康、信心、興趣，這要怎麼數呢？不能數，也不能一個一個算，這種名詞，就叫做抽象名詞。相信聰明的你，一定很快就學會了吧！

③. 可數名詞和不可數名詞

名詞根據是否能夠計算，可以分為可數名詞和不可數名詞。

1. 可數名詞

可以用數字一個一個數出來的名詞，就叫做可數名詞。可數名詞可以分為單數和複數兩種形式。

單數名詞指的是名詞的數量為「一」，只有一個的東西，例如a book（一本書），a student（一個學生）。

複數名詞是指名詞的數量「大於一」，表示很多個東西，例如two books（兩本書），four students（四個學生）。

在英文中，單數名詞用名詞原形表示。複數名詞則有以下的變化形式：

1. 一般情況→ 詞尾+s

名詞	單數	複數	讀音變化
cap　帽子	cap	caps	無聲子音後讀/s/
team　隊伍	team	teams	有聲子音後讀/z/
car　汽車	car	cars	母音後讀/z/

2. 詞尾是s、x、sh、ch的詞→ 詞尾+es

名詞	單數	複數	讀音變化
bus　公車	bus	buses	
fox　狐狸	fox	foxes	/iz/
dish　菜	dish	dishes	

3. "子音字母+y" 結尾的詞→ 變y為i，再加-es

名詞	單數	複 數	讀音變化
jelly　果凍	jelly	jellies	
lily　百合花	lily	lilies	/z/
baby　嬰兒	baby	babies	

4. 部分詞尾是o的詞→ 詞尾+es

名詞	單數	複 數	讀音變化
potato　馬鈴薯	potato	potatoes	/z/
hero　英雄	hero	heroes	

5. 詞尾是f或fe的詞→ 變f或fe為v，再加-es

名詞	單數	複 數	讀音變化
knife　小刀	knife	knives	/z/
half　一半	half	halves	

要注意喔！

以下特殊變化，請特別記起來：

1. 有些以o結尾的名詞要變成複數時，要直接加-s。如：
   photo → photos（照片）
   piano → pianos（鋼琴）

2. 有些以o結尾的名詞要變成複數時，加-es或者-s都可以。以oo結尾的名詞變 複數時， 要直接加-s。如：
   zero→ zeros / zeroes （零）
   zoo→ zoos （動物園）

3. 有些以f結尾的名詞變成複數時，要直接加-s。如：
   roof→ roofs （屋頂）

有些名詞的複數形式不是以加-s或-es構成，它們的變化是不規則的形態，需要我們一個一個分別去記憶。如：

1. 改變中間母音

例詞	單數	複數
man 男人	man	men
woman 女人	woman	women
goose 鵝	goose	geese
foot 腳	foot	feet
tooth 牙齒	tooth	teeth

2. 字尾加-en或加-ren

例詞	單數	複數
child 兒童	child	children
ox 公牛	ox	oxen

3. 單複數形式相同

例詞	單數	複數
deer 鹿	deer	deer
fish 魚	fish	fish
sheep 綿羊	sheep	sheep
Chinese 中國人	Chinese	Chinese

2. 不可數名詞

不可以用數字一個一個數出來的名詞，就叫做不可數名詞。不可數名詞沒有單複數的區分。

不可數名詞的特徵：

1. 不可數名詞在句子中一般被視為單數。如：

There is some tea in the cup.
杯子裡面有茶。

I want to buy some rice.
我想買一些米。

2. 不可數名詞前面不能用a或an，但可以用the。如：

The milk on the table is for you.
桌子上的牛奶是給你的。

The bread tastes good.
這個麵包很好吃。

3. 表示一類事物的不可數名詞在句中作主語時，這時候，動詞要用單數形式。
如：

Glass is an important material.
玻璃是一種重要的材料。

Iron is hard.
鐵很硬。

4. 表示兩類以上事物的不可數名詞作主語時，動詞要用複數形式。如：

Meat and fish are in the fridge.
肉和魚在冰箱裡。

Air and water are important to life.
空氣和水對生命很重要。

➡ **不可數名詞的數量表示：**

　　不可數名詞沒有單複數的區分，但是我們可以借助名詞，來表示它們的量。
如：

She ate a bar of chocolate.
她吃了一塊巧克力。

Mom has bought me two tubes of toothpaste.
媽媽買了兩支牙膏給我。

要注意喔！

隨著學習愈來愈深入，你會發現，英語和中文在表示名
詞的數量時，不僅在書寫的形式上有很多不同，而且在
可數名詞和不可數名詞的劃分上也有一定差別。

4. 名詞的所有格

名詞中表示所有關係的形式叫做名詞的所有格，意思就是「……的」。

所有格有兩種形式：一種是在名詞後面加-'s，通常是用來修飾有生命的東西，如Kate's dress（凱特的洋裝）；另一種是在介系詞 of 後面加名詞，多用來修飾沒有生命的東西，如 the window of the room（房間的窗戶）。

-'s 格

如果名詞代表的事物是有生命的，那麼它的所有格形式就是在這個名詞後面加**-'s**。如：

The boy's father is a lawyer.
這個男孩的父親是一名律師。

That is the Smiths' house.
那是史密斯家的房子。

名詞變為**-'s**的所有格形式，有一定的規則：

1. 一般單數名詞→詞尾+「's」

Jim's sister
吉姆的妹妹

the boy's bike
男孩的腳踏車

2. 詞尾不是s的複數名詞→詞尾+「's」

the children's balls
孩子們的球

the people's rights
人民的權利

3. 詞尾是s的複數名詞→詞尾+「'」

the teachers' books
老師們的書

the kids' crayons
孩子們的蠟筆

4. 在表示店鋪、教堂等或某人的家時，所有格-'s後面通常不出現它所修飾的名詞。

the barber's
理髮店

the Whites'
懷特家

5. 兩個人分別擁有某物時，要在每個人的名字後面加-'s；兩個人共同擁有某物時，只在最後一個人的名字後面加-'s。

Lily's and Mary's rooms
表示莉莉和瑪麗，一人各擁有一個房間

Lily and Mary's room
表示莉莉和瑪麗共同擁有一個房間

of 格

如果名詞代表的事物是沒有生命的，常用of 組成短語來表示它的所有格。如：

The name of the cartoon is *Cinderella*.
這部卡通的名字是《灰姑娘》。

the first lesson of this semester
這學期的第一堂課

要注意喔！

在表示「某人的照片」時，**of** 後面要接有生命的事物。如：

a photo of an old woman 一張老太太的照片

1. 請將下列名詞分類（在正確的對應處打 "✓"）。

類別 名詞	人	動物	地點	物品	抽象概念
Catherine	✓				
power					
wine					
painting					
rabbit					
classroom					
joy					
mother					
London					
goose					
truth					
raincoat					
bookshop					
doctor					
elephant					

2. 判斷下列句子中套色的字是不是專有名詞（如果是，在這個專有名詞下畫線）。

例 <u>Amy</u> lives in this building.

艾咪住在這棟房子裏。

1. Mr. Green is Lily's father.

2. The children go to school by bike.

3. Miss Brown is a nurse.

4. I enjoy myself at Christmas.

5. Her hometown is London.

3. 判斷下列句中套色的字是否是不可數名詞，如果是，在括號內填 "Y"，如果不是則填 "N"。

例 I want two bowls (N) of rice (Y) .

我想要兩碗飯。

1. I bought Dad a can (　　) of beer (　　) .

2. Do you know Alice's telephone (　　) number (　　) ?

3. Is the ring (　　) made of gold (　　) ?

4. There is a fish (　　) in the water (　　) .

5. The Chinese (　　) love tea (　　) .

4. 請寫出下列名詞的複數形式。

例 cap　<u>caps</u>

1. telephone____	2. fish____	3. ring____	4. rice____
5. fox____	6. woman____	7. child____	8. sheep____
9. girl____	10. glass____	11. knife____	12. foot____

5. 根據中文意思寫出下面詞語的所有格。

例 婦女節 the Women Day

the <u>Women's</u> Day

1. 麵包房 the baker

_____

2. 那個男孩的名字 that boy name

_____

3. 喬的眼鏡 Joe glasses

_____

4. 臥室的門 the door the bedroom

_____

5. 屋頂的顏色 the color the roof

_____

你做對了嗎？

1.

名詞 ＼ 類別	人	動物	地點	物品	抽象概念
Catherine	✓				
power					✓
wine				✓	
painting				✓	
rabbit		✓			
classroom			✓		
joy					✓
mother	✓				
London			✓		
goose		✓			
truth					✓
raincoat				✓	
bookshop			✓		
doctor	✓				
elephant		✓			

2.	1. 畫線：<u>Mr. Green</u> is Lily's father.（格林先生是莉莉的父親。）
	2. 不畫線：The children go to school by bike.
	3. 不畫線：Miss Brown is a nurse.
	4. 畫線：I enjoy myself at <u>Christmas</u>.（聖誕節我玩得很開心。）
	5. 畫線：Her hometown is <u>London</u>.（她的家鄉是倫敦。）

3.	1. N;Y（我買了一罐啤酒給爸爸。）
	2. N;N（你知道愛麗絲的電話號碼嗎？）
	3. N;Y（這個戒指是黃金做的嗎？）
	4. N;Y（水裏有條魚。）
	5. N;Y（中國人喜歡喝茶。）

4.	1. telephones	2. fish/fishes	3. rings	4. rice（不可數）
	5. foxes	6. women	7. children	8. sheep（單複數同型）
	9. girls	10. glasses	11. knives	12. feet

5.	1. the baker's
	2. that boy's name
	3. Joe's glasses
	4. the door of the bedroom
	5. the color of the roof

♥ 確實了解每一題後，再進行下一章喔！

Unit 2.
冠詞

Unit 2. 冠詞

❶ 什麼是冠詞？

冠詞是出現在名詞前面，為這個名詞設定範圍的詞。

英語中的冠詞一共有三個：a、an、the，其中 a 和 an 是不定冠詞，the 是定冠詞。

要注意喔！

冠詞本身沒有意義，不能離開名詞單獨使用，只能和名詞連用。

❷ 不定冠詞

不定冠詞 a、an 沒有特別指定某些東西，通常泛指同類事物中的某一個（或某一位、枝、塊、片……）。其中，a 用在以子音開頭的名詞前，如 a book（一本書）；an 用在以母音（a、e、i、o、u）開頭的名詞前，如 an apple（一個蘋果）。

1. 不定冠詞的主要用法

1. 相當於數量詞「1」。

There are seven days in a week.
一週有七天。

There are sixty minutes in an hour.（注意：hour為母音開頭的字）
一小時有60分鐘。

2. 統稱一類人或物。

A bird can fly.
鳥會飛。（全部的鳥都會飛。）

An elephant likes bananas.
大象喜歡吃香蕉。（＝全部的大象都喜歡吃香蕉。）

3. 泛指一類名詞中的某一個。

Tom is an actor.
湯姆是一名演員。

He bought me a new bike.
他買了一輛新的腳踏車給我。

4. 有一些習慣用語中也會出現。

a little 一點點	for a while 一下子
in a word 總而言之	have a try 試一試

要注意喔！

1. 有些名詞的字首雖然是母音字母（ a、e、i、o、u ），但是名詞的發音卻以子音開頭。這時名詞前要用 **a**。如：

   a university [ˌjunəˋvɝsətɪ] 一所大學

   a uniform [ˋjunəˏfɔrm] 一套制服

   university 和 uniform 的單字字首「u」唸起來像是 [ju]，是子音，所以這種時候就要用 **a** 來當冠詞。

2. 有些名詞的字首是雖然是子音字母，但名詞發音卻以母音開頭。這時名詞前要用**an**。如：

   an hour [aʊr] 一小時

   an honor [ˋɑnə] 一項榮譽

   雖然 hour 和 honor 的單字字首「h」是子音，但它們唸起來是 [aʊ]、[ɑ]，所以才會用 **an** 當冠詞。

3. 定冠詞

定冠詞 the 通常對所修飾的名詞有指定作用，表示「這個、那個、這些、那些」。

1. 定冠詞的主要用法

1. 用於特定的人或物前面。

The girl in red is my sister.
那個穿紅衣服的女孩是我姐姐。

The ruler on the box is mine.
盒子上的尺是我的。

2. 講到前一段文字提到過的人或事時使用。

I have a book. The book is on the desk.
我有一本書。那本書在桌子上。

Tom saw a film last night. The film was about animals.
湯姆昨天晚上看了一場電影。那場電影跟動物有關。

3. 用於獨一無二的事物前面。

The sun is bigger than the moon.
太陽比月亮大。

A bird is flying high in the sky.
一隻鳥在空中高高飛翔。

4. 用於形容詞前，表示某一類的人。

The poor don't have enough to eat.
窮人沒有足夠的東西可以吃。

We should help the blind.
我們應該幫助盲人。

5. 用於序數詞、形容詞最高級及形容詞 only、very、same 等詞前面。（有關形容詞最高級是什麼，後面的Unit 4 有更詳細的說明喔！）

May is the fifth month.
五月是第五個月份。（fifth為序數詞）

Mary is the youngest teacher in our school.
瑪麗是我們學校最年輕的老師。

I have the same idea.
我有相同的看法。

6. 用於某些由普通名詞構成的國家、單位、機關團體、階級等專有名詞前。

the United Kingdom 英國

the United States 美國

7. 用於表示樂器的名詞前。

She can play the piano.
她會彈鋼琴。

Tony is good at playing the violin.
東尼擅長拉小提琴。

8. 放在姓氏的複數名詞之前,就可以表示「XXX 一家人」。

The Whites are visiting London.
懷特一家正在倫敦遊覽。

The Smiths are watching a football game.
史密斯一家在看足球賽。

9. 用於習慣用語中。

I often do some shopping in the afternoon.
我常常下午去買東西。

In the middle of the night, they finally reached that town.
半夜,他們終於抵達了那個城鎮。

要注意喔!

the 在母音前讀 [ðɪ];在子音前讀 [ðə]。如:
The [ðɪ] air was full of butterflies. 空中都是蝴蝶。
The [ðə] book is mine. 這本書是我的。

4. 不用冠詞的情況

在某些情況下,名詞前面可以不用加冠詞。

1. 不用冠詞的幾種情況

1. 國名、人名等專有名詞前通常不用冠詞。
England 英格蘭 **Mary** 瑪麗

2. 複數名詞泛指很多個同一類的人或事物時，可以不用冠詞。

They are boxes.
它們是盒子。

3. 不可數名詞前通常不加不定冠詞 a、an（因為它們不可數，當然也不會有「一個」的狀況了），但可以用定冠詞 the 修飾。

Water is important to us.
水對我們來說很重要。

Where is the milk?
牛奶在哪裡？

4. 在表示季節、月份、星期等表示時間的名詞前，不加冠詞。

We go to school from Monday to Friday.
我們禮拜一到禮拜五去上學。

5. 在稱呼或表示官銜、職位的名詞前不加冠詞。

This is President Wang.
這是王總統。

6. 在表示三餐、球類運動和娛樂運動的名詞前，不加冠詞。
have breakfast 吃早餐　**play basketball** 打籃球　**play chess** 下棋

7. 當兩類或兩個以上名詞一起用時，常把冠詞省掉。

I can't write without pen or pencil.
沒有鋼筆和鉛筆，我就不能寫字。

8. 冠詞通常不跟其他的修飾詞一起使用。
這是我的書。

This is my book. (o)

This is my a book. (×)

9. 在一些慣用的介詞短語中不用冠詞。

by bike 騎腳踏車去	**in hospital** 在醫院
in bed 在床上	**at night** 在夜裡

1. 以下空格應該填入 a 還是 an 呢？看看名詞的開頭是子音還是母音，就可以判斷了喔！

例 I have __a__ book.

我有一本書。

1. Jerry's mother is _____ teacher.

2. Mary is _____ clever girl.

3. There is _____ fish in the water.

4. I have _____ apple.

2. 把正確的答案圈起來。如果覺得不需要填任何東西，則圈「/」。

例 Lily is ((a,) an, the) serious child.

莉莉是一個嚴肅的孩子。

1. Is (the, /) Tom (a, the, /) tallest boy in our team?

2. She has (a, an, the) iPhone. (A, The) iPhone is white.

3. Is (the, /) Mary (a, the, /) youngest girl in our class?

4. Can you play (a, an, the) violin?

5. (An, The) outside of (a, an, the) house was painted red.

♥ 下一頁還有題目喔！

3. 根據這章學到的內容，在空格上填入正確的字吧！

> a   an   the   ✕

My name is ___✕___ Michael. I'm in ___1___ Grade Three this semester. My mother is ___2___ doctor and my father is ___3___ actor. Today is ___4___ Saturday.

Now, my father is talking on ___5___ phone. My mother is having ___6___ breakfast. My grandmother is watering ___7___ flowers in ___8___ garden and I'm watching ___9___ TV.

Look! This is my room. There is ___10___ umbrella in my bedroom. I like ___11___ umbrella very much because my father bought it for me in ___12___ Paris. These are all my presents. My father buys me a lot of presents every year from all over the world.

中譯：

　　我的名字是麥可。我這學期三年級了。我的媽媽是一位醫生，而我爸爸是一位演員。今天是星期六。

　　我爸爸現在在講電話，我媽媽正在吃早餐，我奶奶在花園澆花，而我正在看電視。

　　看！這是我的房間。我的臥房裡有一把雨傘。我非常喜歡這把雨傘因為我爸爸是在巴黎買給我的。這些都是我的禮物，我爸爸每年都會從世界各地買很多禮物給我。

參考解答

你做對了嗎？

1.	1. a （傑瑞的媽媽是一位老師。）
	2. a （瑪麗是一個聰明的女孩。）
	3. a （水中有一條魚。）
	4. an （我有一個蘋果。）

2.	1. / ; the （湯姆是我們團隊裡最高的男孩嗎？）
	2. an ; The （她有一支 iPhone。那支 iPhone 是白色的。）
	3. / ; the （瑪麗是我們班年紀最小的女生嗎？）
	4. the （你會拉小提琴嗎？）
	5. The ; the （這棟房子的外牆被刷成了紅色。）

| 3. | 1. ✕ 2. a 3. an 4. ✕ 5. the 6. ✕ |
| | 7. the 8. the 9. ✕ 10. an 11. the 12. ✕ |

♥ 確實了解每一題後，再進行下一章喔！

Unit 3.
代名詞

Unit 3. 代名詞

1. 什麼是代名詞？

　　代名詞，顧名思義就是用來代替名詞的詞。有時候不只代替名詞一個單字而已，也可能代替具有名詞詞性的短語、子句或整個句子。在中文裡，也有這樣的用法。譬如當我們聊天聊到某一個人，一直稱呼他的名字可能太麻煩，我們會用「他／她」來表示，英文也是如此。換句話說，句子中本來應該出現名詞的地方，為了避免反覆出現同一個字，我們就可以使用「代名詞」。看看以下的例句：

You must not play with the match. Give it to me.
不准玩火柴。把它給我。（這裡的代名詞 it 是用來代替名詞 the match。）

This is our dog. Its name is Lucky.
這是我們的狗。牠的名字叫來福。
（這裡的代名詞 its 是用來代替名詞短語 our dog。）

I had a talk with my English teacher. It was very helpful.
我和我的英語老師聊過了。這對我幫助非常大。
（這裡的代名詞 it 代替前面的整個句子，代表「我和英文老師聊天」這整件事。）

　　代名詞可以分為八類：人稱代名詞、物主代名詞、反身代名詞、指示代名詞、疑問代名詞、不定代名詞、關係代名詞、相互代名詞。我們先來看看前面六種代名詞是怎麼回事吧！

2. 人稱代名詞

　　在講一個人的事時，一直講他的名字很累吧？所以才會有人稱代名詞這種東西出現。人稱代名詞可以避免重複，用來代替前面提到過的人、動物、事物的名稱。如：

Lisa and Sharon, Mom is waiting for you!
麗莎、莎倫，媽媽在等你們！
（這裡的代名詞 you 拿來代替名詞 Lisa and Sharon。）

Pick up your toys and put them away.
把你的玩具撿起來，把它們收好。
（這裡的代名詞 them 代替名詞 your toys。）

人稱代名詞，依其代替的人稱、單、複數或主格與受格而有不同：

數\格\人稱	單數		複數	
	主格	受格	主格	受格
第一人稱	I 我	me	we 我們	us
第二人稱	you 你	you	you 你們	you
第三人稱	he 他 she 她 it 它	him her it	they 他們	them

要注意喔！

1. 在一個句子裡的動詞之前出現，要用「主格」的代名詞，如：**I**、**you**、**they**，在動詞之後，則要用「受格」的代名詞，如：**me**、**us**、**them**。

2. 說話的人本身就是第一人稱（我）；正在聽他講話的人是第二人稱（你）；聊到所有其他人（或動物、物品）時，就是第三人稱（他、她、它）。

1. 人稱代名詞的基本用法

1. 人稱代名詞可以做為句子裡面的主詞。

I am a student.
我是個學生。

Good morning, boys and girls. You may sit down now.
早安，孩子們，現在你們可以坐下了。

2. 人稱代名詞也可以做為句子裡面的受詞。

We can help them.
我們能幫他們。（help是動詞，在動詞後面要用受詞them，不能用they）

It's a present for me.
這是給我的禮物。

"Who's that?"　　　　**"It's me."**
「誰啊？」　　　　　　「是我。」

2. 第三人稱代名詞中「it」的基本用法

1. 拿來代替前面已經提過的事物（不需再重覆一次）。

"Where is the puppy?"　　　　**"It's over there."**
「小狗狗在哪？」　　　　　　　「牠在那邊。」

2. 拿來代替性別不明的嬰兒或動物（因為不知道性別，不能說 he 或 she）。

It's a lovely baby. Is it a boy or a girl?
這寶寶真可愛。它是男孩還是女孩？

3. 代替不確定的人或事物。

"Who is it?"　　　　**"It's me."**
「誰啊？」　　　　　「是我。」

4. 用來表示時間、距離和自然現象等比較抽象的東西。

What time is it by your watch?
你的錶現在幾點了？

"How's the weather today?"　　　　**"It's rainy."**
「今天天氣怎樣？」　　　　　　　　「下雨啊。」

要注意喔！

1. 表示「我」的人稱代名詞 I 一定是大寫！沒有人會說 i am happy 的！

2. 英語中表示「我和你」、「我們和你們」時，第一人稱放在後面。如：

you and me 你和我

you and us 你們和我們

③. 物主代名詞

　　物主代名詞是表示「擁有」、「屬於」關係的代名詞，就像中文裡面會説「我的」、「你的」、「他的」一樣。例如：

My father is a dentist.
我的父親是牙醫。

Sally wrote a letter to her aunt.
莎莉寫了一封信給她的姑姑。

　　物主代名詞可分為形容詞和名詞兩種用法，其人稱和單複數表示也有不同：

數　　　人稱　類別	單數			複數		
	第一人稱	第二人稱	第三人稱	第一人稱	第二人稱	第三人稱
形容詞性物主代名詞	my 我的	your 你的	his 他的 her 她的 its 它的	our 我們的	your 你們的	their 他們的
名詞性物主代名詞	mine 我的	yours 你的	his 他的 her 她的 its 它的	our 我們的	yours 你們的	theirs 他們的

1. 物主代詞的基本用法

1. 形容詞性物主代名詞後面一定要接一個名詞，因為它是用來「形容」一個名詞是屬於誰的。

   This is my camera.
   這是我的相機。（camera 是名詞）

   His sister is a nurse.
   他的姐姐是一名護士。（sister 也是名詞）

2. 名詞性物主代名詞本身就有名詞的性質，可以用來代替「形容詞性物主代詞＋名詞」。

   These apples are yours. Ours are in the basket.
   這些蘋果是你們的。我們的在籃子裡。

   (yours = your apples　　　ours = our apples)

I've lost my pen. May I use yours?
我的鋼筆丟了。我可以用你的嗎？　　**(yours = your pen)**

This book is mine.
這本書是我的。　　　**(mine = my book)**

④. 反身代名詞

表示「我自己」、「你自己」、「他自己」、「我們自己」、「你們自己」和「他們自己」等的代名詞，叫做反身代名詞。反身代名詞的主要形式是：

人稱	單數	複數
第一人稱	myself 我自己	ourselves 我們自己
第二人稱	yourself 你自己	yourselves 你們自己
第三人稱	himself 他自己 herself 她自己 itself 它自己	themselves 他們自己
不定人稱	oneself 某人自己	

1. 反身代名詞的基本用法

1. 一個句子中的主詞跟受詞都是同一個人時，用反身代名詞。

You should take good care of yourself.
你要好好照顧自己。

Adam hurt himself while he was cutting things.
亞當切東西的時候，傷到了自己。

2. 強調語氣時，用反身代名詞。

I can do it myself.
我自己可以做。

Judy cooked dinner herself.
茱蒂自己做晚飯。

要注意喔！

1. 單數反身代名詞的詞尾都是 **-self**，複數反身代名詞的詞尾都是 **-selves**。

2. 反身代詞本身沒有所有格，所以如果要講「我自己的」、「你自己的」、「他自己的」等，要用**own**來代替，可以加強句子的語氣。如：

He made it with his own hands.
這是他用自己的雙手做的。

5. 指示代名詞

指示代名詞是表示「這個」、「那個」、「這些」、「那些」等指示人或事物的代名詞。指示代名詞有 this、that、these、those等。如：

This is my home.
這是我的家。

That is my grandpa.
那是我爺爺。

These are my toys.
這些是我的玩具。

Those are students.
那些人是學生。

1. 指示代名詞的基本用法

1. 指示代名詞分為單數與複數兩種形式：

指示代名詞	數量	用法
this/that 這個／那個	單數	後面接動詞的單數形式
these/those 這些／那些	複數	後面接動詞的複數形式

This is a bed.
這是一張床。
（因為 this 是單數，後面就接單數形式的動詞 is。）

That is a tree.
那是一棵樹。
（因為 that 是單數，後面就接單數形式的動詞 is。）

These are horses.
這些是馬。
（因為 these 是複數，後面就接複數形式的動詞 are。）

Those are ducks.
那些是鴨子。
（因為 those 是複數，後面就接複數形式的動詞 is。）

2. 指示代名詞在可以指比較遠的東西，也可以指比較近的東西。

　　this 和 these指空間上較近的事物；that 和 those 指空間上較遠的事物。如：

This is my bike.
這是我的腳踏車。

That is your bike.
那是你的腳踏車。

These are my books.
這些是我的書。

Those are her books.
那些是她的書。

3. this 和 that 可以用來代替之前說過的話。

Miss Green is a very good teacher. That is why we like her very much.
格林小姐是位好老師。這就是我們非常喜歡她的原因。
（用 that 代替 Miss Green is a very good teacher 這件事）

I didn't finish my homework. This made Miss Green angry.
我功課沒寫完。這讓格林小姐很生氣。
（用 this 代替 I didn't finish my homework 這件事）

⑥ 疑問代名詞

　　要問「誰？」、「什麼東西？」等問題時，就用疑問代名詞。疑問代名詞有 who（誰，主格）、whom（誰，受格）、whose（誰的）、which（哪一個）和 what（什麼）等。

疑問代名詞		替代範圍
who	誰（主格）	人
whom	誰（受格）	
whose	誰的	
which	哪一個	人、事、物
what	什麼	事、物

1. 疑問代名詞的基本用法

1. who（誰）：在句中當主詞，只能用於對人的提問。

Who is he?
他是誰？

Who knows the teacher?
誰認識那個老師？

2. whom（誰）：whom 是 who 的受詞形式。

Who(m) did you see in the street?
你在街上看到誰了？

Who(m) are you talking about?
你們在討論誰？

3. whose（誰的）：詢問東西的主人是誰時用。

Whose books are these on the desk?
桌上的這些書是誰的？

Whose umbrella is this?
這是誰的傘？

4. which（哪一個）：問到關於人、事或物的問題時都可以用。

Which is bigger, the green one or the yellow one?
哪一個比較大，綠色的還是黃色的？

Which way did they go?
他們往哪裡走了？

5. what（什麼）：可用於對事或物的提問。

What happened?
發生什麼事了？

What are they doing?
他們在做什麼？

What day is it today?
今天是星期幾？

7. 不定代名詞

不指明是代替哪個特定名詞或形容詞的代名詞，叫做不定代名詞。例如下面這些情況，這些代名詞都沒有特定指哪個東西：

Is there anything I can do?
我能做點什麼嗎？

Did you hear something?
你有沒有聽到什麼？

Many of them are from Britain.
他們當中有很多人來自英國。

Both of the apples are red.
這兩個蘋果都是紅的。

1. some、any和no的用法

some 和 any 都有「一些」的意思；no 則表示「沒有」的意思。

1. some 通常用於肯定句中，any 用於否定句或疑問句中。例如：

There is some bread left.
還有剩一點麵包。

Do you have any crayons?
你有蠟筆嗎？

Yes, I have some.
有，我有一些。　　**(some = some crayons)**

No, I don't have any.
沒有，我沒有蠟筆。**(any = any crayons)**

Ken doesn't have any pets.
肯沒有養任何寵物。

2. no 用在肯定句中表示否定的意思。如：

There are no letters for you today.
今天沒有你的信。

要注意喔！

1. 在 **"Would you like..."** 的疑問句中，一般用 **some**，不用 **any**。如：
Would you like some juice?
你想要一些果汁嗎？

2. **any** 用於肯定句時，表示「任何」的意思。如：
Here are three storybooks. You may read any of them.
這裡有三本故事書。你可以讀任何一本沒關係。

2. some-、any-、no- 開頭的詞的用法

由 some-、any-、no- 開頭的詞，用法也和 some、any、no 相同。例如：

someone 某人	somebody 某人	something 某事物
anyone 任何人	anybody 任何人	anything 任何事物
no one 沒有人	nobody 沒有人	nothing 沒有事物

Someone took my doll!
有人拿走了我的洋娃娃！

Did you tell anyone the news?
你有把消息告訴任何人嗎？

No one knows the answer.
沒有人知道答案。

Somebody is sure to get interested in this activity.
一定有人對這個活動感興趣。

Is there anybody at home?
有任何人在家嗎？

Nobody knew her name.
沒有人知道她的名字。

There is something wrong with Jim.
吉姆出了點問題。

I will do anything for you.
我願意為你做任何事。

There is nothing important.
沒有什麼重要的事。

3. both 和 all 的用法

　　both 和 all 都有「都……」的意思，表示「整體」。這兩個有什麼差別呢？

1. both 表示「兩個都……」，後面如果接動詞，要用複數形式。如：

Both of the boys are clever.
這兩個男孩都很聰明。

Both of Lucy's parents are doctors.
露西的父母兩人都是醫生。

2. all 表示「三個以上都……」，後面如果接複數名詞時，動詞就用複數形式；後面如果接不可數名詞，動詞就用單數形式。如：

All the milk is gone.
全部的牛奶都沒了。（milk 是不可數名詞，所以用單數動詞 is）

All of the students like P.E.
所有的學生都愛上體育課。

4. every 和 each 的用法

　　every 和 each 都有「每個」的意思。那同樣是「每個」，它們和 both 與 all 有什麼差別呢？差別在於 both 和 all 代表的是「整體」，而 every 和 each 都有「個體」、「各個」的含義。

1. every 表示「各個」，有「整體之中的每一個」的含義，後面接的動詞用單數形式。如：

   Every pupil got a book.
   每個小學生都各拿到了一本書。

   Every boy and every girl is smart.
   每個男孩和每個女孩都很聰明。

2. each 表示「每個」，強調個體，後面接的動詞用單數形式。如：

   Each kid has a toy.
   每個孩子各都有一個玩具。

   Each of them has a mobile phone.
   他們每個人都各有一支手機。

要注意喔！

every- 與 -body, -one, -thing 組合，就會構成新的單詞。everybody 與 everyone 表示「每一個人」，everything 表示「每一件事」。後面接的動詞要用單數。例如：

Everyone likes Susan very much.
每一個人都非常喜歡蘇珊。

Everybody has some weak spot.
每個人都有個什麼弱點。

Everything is going well with me.
我一切都很好。

5. either 和 neither 的用法

either 和 neither 的意義相反。它們的差別在哪裡呢？

1. either 指「兩個中的任何一個都……」，後面的動詞用單數形式。如：

   Either of the two boys is clever.
   兩個男孩中的任一個都很聰明。

Either book is interesting.
兩本書的任一本都很有趣。

2. neither 表示「兩個都不」，後面的動詞用單數形式。如：

Neither of them likes hamburgers.
他們兩個都不喜歡漢堡。

Neither book is interesting.
兩本書都沒意思。

> ### 6. many / much、a few / a little、few / little 的用法

這些都是表示「數量」的不定代詞。它們分別該用在哪裡呢？

1. many 和 much 都有「很多、大量」的意思。many 後面接可數的名詞，much後面接不可數的名詞。例如：

There are many trees around the playground.
操場四周有很多樹。（trees 可數名詞）

Many of them are students.
他們之中有許多人是學生。

Much jam is left.
還剩下很多果醬。（jam 不可數名詞）

Much of what you say is not true.
你說的有很多都不是真的。

2. a few 和 a little 都有「少數、少量」的意思。a few 後面接可數的名詞，a little後面接不可數的名詞。例如：

I have a few books.
我有幾本書。（books 可數名詞）

Only a few children can read.
只有幾個孩子識字。

She has a little time.
她有一點點時間。（time 不可數名詞）

How much is left? Only a little.
還剩多少？只剩下一點點。

3. few 和 little 都有「幾乎沒有」的意思。few 後面接可數名詞，little 後面接不可數名詞。例如：

Jim has few friends.
吉姆幾乎沒什麼朋友。

There are few apples left.
快沒蘋果了。

There's little butter in the plate.
盤子裡幾乎沒有奶油。

We have little food left in the fridge.
我們冰箱裡沒剩什麼食物了。

不定代名詞	中文
many + 可數名詞 much + 不可數名詞	很多、大量
a few + 可數名詞 a little + 不可數名詞	一些
few + 可數名詞 little + 不可數名詞	幾乎沒有

要注意喔！

a few / a little 是肯定的，意思是「還有一點點」，而 **few / little** 有否定的意思，意思是「幾乎沒有」。例如：

He has a few friends. 他有幾個朋友。（肯定）

He has few friends. 他幾乎沒有朋友。（否定）

（friends是可數名詞，所以用a few / few）

We still have a little time. 我們還有點時間。（肯定）

There is little time left. 幾乎沒剩下什麼時間了。（否定）

（time是不可數名詞，所以用a little / little）

1. 用正確的人稱代名詞填空看看吧！

例 What can __I__ do for __you__ , sir?
先生，我能為您做點什麼嗎？

1. My name is Tony. _____ come from America.

2. Meimei and Lily are friends and _____ like dancing.

3. Are _____ ready, David?

4. Miss White teaches us English and _____ enjoy the lessons very much.

5. _____ is half past seven now.

6. My mother is a teacher and _____ likes her job very much.

7. My father is a policeman and _____ has a gun.

8. Where are my keys? I can't find _____.

9. The prince walked up to Cinderella and asked _____ for a dance.

10. _____ is very cold here in winter.

2. 用正確的代名詞填填看！

例 Tony cleans __his__ room every Friday.
東尼每週五會打掃房間。

1. _____ pencil is broken. I need to buy a new one.

2. What is _____ father, Jerry?

3. Mary, this is my chair. _____ is over there.

4. Meimei is a good girl and _____ likes helping others.

5. I am a teacher. This is _____ student.

6. Boys and girls, open _____ books and turn to Page 26.

7. Fred is a friend of _____. We often invite him to dinner.

8. We grew an apple tree in front of _____ house.

9. The young couple is too busy to look after _____ baby.

10. Tom never wears a watch, so this watch can't be _____.

3. 請從下面的字中選出適當的反身代名詞，填到空格中吧！

| yourselves | itself | myself | himself |
| herself | themselves | yourself | ourselves |

例 **I cooked the dish _myself_ .**
這菜是我自己做的。

1. Bob hurt _____ in the car accident.

2. "Can I help you, Judy?" "No, thank you. I can manage it _____."

3. Children, you must do the homework _____.

4. Alice is not quite _____ today.

5. Help _____ to some chicken soup, Betty.

6. Mom and Dad are going on holiday, and we have to look after _____.

7. Look! The cat is washing _____.

8. They painted the house all by _____.

4. 根據中文提示，填入適當的指示代名詞，把句子補充完整吧！

> 例 這是凱特的書包。
>
> ___This___ is Kate's bag.

1. 這是一隻斑馬。

   _____ is a zebra.

2. 那是一隻袋鼠。

   _____ is a kangaroo.

3. 這些是山羊，那些是綿羊。

   _____ are goats. _____ are sheep.

4. 妳好，露西！這是我的同學凱西。

   Hello, Lucy! _____ is my classmate Cathy.

5. 喂，我是湯姆，你是大衛嗎？

   Hello, this is Tom. Is _____ David?

6. 喂，請問你是哪位？

   Hello. Who is _____ speaking, please?

7. 「那邊那個女孩是誰？」
   「那是莉莉。」

   "Who is the girl over there?"

   "_____ is Lily."

8. 這邊走，請！

   _____ way, please!

9. 約翰沒有通過這次考試。這讓他的老師很生氣。

   John didn't pass the exam. _____ made his teacher very angry.

5. 每一題都有三個選項，從裡面選出適合的疑問代名詞來填空吧！

> 例 ___What___ is your name?
>
> (What, Who, Which)
>
> 你叫什麼名字？

1. _____ do you like better, bananas or apples?

   (What, Which, Whose)

2. "_____ is your father?"

   "He is a doctor."

   (Which, Who, What)

3. "_____ part of Taiwan do you come from?"

   "I come from the south."

   (Which, Who, What)

4. _____ is Miss Green?

   (What, Which, Who)

5. _____ are these crayons?

   (Who, Whose, What)

6. 把正確的不定代詞圈起來！

例 **He has (some , any) teddies.**
他有幾隻玩具熊。

1. There are (some, any) books on her desk.

2. We don't have (some, any) meat in the fridge.

3. The little girl has (many, much) dolls.

4. Would you like (some, any) orange juice?

5. There are trees on (either, both) side of the road.

6. Martha goes jogging (every, each) morning.

7. Please give me (a few, a little) of that drink.

8. (Few, Little) of my friends like carrots.

9. (Both, All) of his parents are teachers.

你做對了嗎？

1.

1. I （我叫東尼。我來自美國。）

2. they （梅梅和莉莉是朋友。她們喜歡跳舞。）

3. you （大衛，你準備好了沒？）

4. we （懷特小姐教我們英文，我們很喜歡上她的課。）

5. It （現在是七點半。）
（half 是「一半」的意思，half past seven 超過7一半了，也就是7點半的意思。）

6. she （我媽媽是一位老師，她很喜歡她的工作。）

7. he （我爸爸是一位警察，他有一把槍。）

8. them （我的鑰匙在哪？我找不到。）

9. her （王子朝灰姑娘走來，邀她跳舞。）

10. It （這邊的冬天很冷。）

2.

1. My （我的鉛筆壞了，我需要買一支新的。）

2. your （傑瑞，你爸爸是做什麼工作的？）
（注意What is your father 不是問「你爸爸是什麼」，而是問從事什麼職業。）

3. Yours （瑪麗，這是我的椅子。妳的在那邊啦。）

4. she （梅梅是個好女孩，她樂於助人。）

5. my （我是個老師，這是我學生。）

6. your （孩子們，把你們的書打開，翻到第 26 頁。）

7. ours （弗雷德是我們的一個朋友。我們經常請他過來吃飯。）

8. our（我們在房子前面種了一棵蘋果樹。）

9. their（這對年輕的夫婦太忙了，沒時間照顧他們的寶寶。）

10. his（湯姆從來不戴手錶，所以這支錶不可能是他的。）

3.	1. himself（鮑伯在車禍中傷了自己。）
	2. myself（「我能幫妳嗎，茱蒂？」「不用，謝謝。我自己來就可以了。」）
	3. yourselves（孩子們，你們的功課要自己寫啊。）
	4. herself（愛麗絲今天不太像她自己。＝愛麗絲今天不太舒服。）
	5. yourself（貝蒂，請自己喝點雞湯吧。）
	6. ourselves（爸爸媽媽要去度假了，我們只好自己照顧自己了。）
	7. itself（你看！貓咪正在幫自己洗澡。）
	8. themselves（他們自己粉刷了房子。）

4.	1. This	2. That	3. These; Those	4. This
	5. that（注意這一題是電話中的對談，在電話用語中問對方是誰，因為看不到對方所以不能說 Are you David? 而要問 Is that David?）			
	6. that	7. That	8. This	9. This

5.	1. Which（你比較喜歡哪一種，香蕉還是蘋果？）
	2. What （你爸爸是做什麼工作的？他是個醫生。）
	3. Which（你是台灣哪裡人？我是南部人。）
	4. Who（誰是格林小姐？）
	5. Whose（這些蠟筆是誰的？）

6.	1. some （她的桌上有幾本書。）
	2. any（我們的冰箱裡一點肉也沒有。）
	3. many（小女孩有好多洋娃娃。）
	4. some（你想要喝點柳橙汁嗎？）
	5. either（馬路的兩側都有樹。）
	6. every（瑪莎每天早晨都去慢跑。）
	7. a little（請給我喝一點點那個飲料。）
	8. Few（我的朋友中沒有幾個喜歡吃胡蘿蔔的。）
	9. Both（他的父母兩人都是老師。）

♥ 確實了解每一題後，再進行下一章喔！

Unit 4.
形容詞

Unit 4. 形容詞

1. 讓我們來認識形容詞

形容詞是用來修飾、描述名詞（或代名詞），表示人或事物的性質、狀態和特徵的詞。如：

John is an honest boy.
約翰是一個誠實的男孩。（形容詞 honest 修飾名詞 boy）

This is a busy street.
這是一條繁忙的大街。（形容詞 busy 修飾名詞 street）

Is there anything wrong?
有什麼問題嗎？（形容詞 wrong 修飾不定代名詞 anything）

Martha is absent because she is ill.
瑪莎不在，因為她生病了。
（形容詞 absent 描述名詞 Martha；形容詞 ill 描述代名詞 she）

2. 形容詞的種類

形容詞根據其構成可分為簡單形容詞和複合形容詞。

簡單形容詞由一個詞構成。如：

long 長的　　　　　　huge 巨大的
blue 藍色的　　　　　bright 明亮的

複合形容詞一般由兩個或兩個以上的詞構成。如：

good-looking 好看的　　hand-made 手工製作的
new-born 新生的　　　　kind-hearted 善良的

要注意喔！

名詞有時也可以拿來修飾另一個名詞，也就是說，雖然是名詞，卻當作形容詞在用。如：

a city boy 一個城市男孩

a paper plane 一架紙飛機

③ 形容詞的位置

1. 形容詞通常用在名詞的前面。

He is a good student.
他是個好學生。（good是形容詞「好的」修飾名詞student「學生」）

She is a famous scientist.
她是位著名的科學家。
（famous是形容詞「有名的」修飾名詞scientist「科學家」）

2. 形容詞也可以用在某些特定動詞的後面。

The dog is smart.
這隻狗很聰明。（is是be動詞，後接形容詞smart「聰明的」）

The leaves turn yellow in autumn.
秋天的樹葉變黃了。（turn是動詞，後接形容詞yellow「黃色的」）

3. 形容詞還可以用在不定代名詞後面，用來修飾不定代名詞。

Cathy found something strange in the magic box.
凱西在魔術盒裡面發現了奇怪的東西。
（形容詞strange「奇怪的」修飾不定代名詞something）

④ 形容詞的排列順序

　　當兩個或兩個以上的形容詞修飾一個名詞時，通常與被修飾的名詞關係更密切、描述更具體的形容詞，要比較靠近被修飾的名詞。如：

a big round plate　一個大圓盤

　　（不定冠詞a＋表示大小的形容詞big＋表示形狀的形容詞round＋名詞plate）

the gray stone bench　這個灰色石椅

　　（定冠詞the＋表示顏色的形容詞gray＋表示材質的形容詞stone＋名詞bench）

her new silk skirt　她的新絲綢裙子

　　（物主代名詞her＋表示新舊的形容詞new＋表示材質的形容詞silk＋名詞skirt）

those tall young Italian men　那些高個子的年輕義大利男人

　　（指示代名詞those＋表示高矮的形容詞tall＋表示年齡的形容詞young＋表示國籍的形容詞Italian＋名詞men）

❺ 形容詞的比較等級

形容詞有三個比較等級：原級、比較級和最高級。

1. 表示「等於」時用原級。如：

She is as tall as I.
她和我一樣高。

2. 一次比較兩個東西時用比較級。如：

She is taller than I.
她比我高。

3. 一次比較三個以上的東西，其中有一個東西「最……」時，用最高級。如：

She is the tallest in our class.
她是我們班最高的。

❻ 形容詞比較級、最高級的構成

形容詞比較級的構成有如下變化：

1. 一般單音節的形容詞和少數雙音節的形容詞

比較級：詞尾+ er

最高級：詞尾+ est

原級	比較級	最高級
tall 高的	taller 更高的	tallest 最高的
clean 乾淨的	cleaner 更乾淨的	cleanest 最乾淨的
clever 聰明的	cleverer 更聰明的	cleverest 最聰明的

2. 以 e 結尾的單音節詞

比較級：詞尾e + r

最高級：詞尾e + st

（只要想著字尾的e共用，就很容易記了！）

原級	比較級	最高級
brave 勇敢的	braver 更勇敢的	bravest 最勇敢的
large 巨大的	larger 更巨大的	largest 最巨大的
safe 安全的	safer 更安全的	safest 最安全的

3. 以「子音字母+ y」結尾的詞

比較級：去 y 加-ier

最高級：去 y 加-iest

原級	比較級	最高級
dry 乾的	drier 更乾的	driest 最乾的
happy 快樂的	happier 更快樂的	happiest 最快樂的
easy 容易的	easier 更容易的	easiest 最容易的

4. 以重音音節結尾，而且結尾的地方只有一個子音字母的詞

比較級：最後一個字母寫兩次+ er

最高級：最後一個字母寫兩次+ est

原級	比較級	最高級
big 大的	bigger 更大的	biggest 最大的
hot 熱的	hotter 更熱的	hottest 最熱的
wet 濕的	wetter 更濕的	wettest 最濕的

5. 有兩個或兩個以上音節的詞

比較級：形容詞的前面+ more

最高級：形容詞的前面+ most

原級	比較級	最高級
beautiful 漂亮的 (beau-ti-ful)	more beautiful 更漂亮的	most beautiful 更漂亮的
useful 有用的 (u-se-ful)	more useful 更有用的	most useful 更有用的
expensive 昂貴的 (ex-pen-sive)	more expensive 更昂貴的	most expensive 更昂貴的

6. 不規則的形容詞變化

有些形容詞比較級的變化是不規則的，需要特別記憶：

原級	比較級	最高級
good / well 好的	better 更好的	best 最好的
bad / ill 壞的	worse 更壞的	worst 最壞的
many / much 多的	more 更多的	most 最多的
few / little 少的	less 更少的	least 最少的
far 遠的	farther / further 更遠的	farthest / furthest 最遠的
old 老的	older / elder 更老的	oldest / eldest 最老的

7. 形容詞的比較等級怎麼用？

1. 形容詞的原級

形容詞的原級如果用來比較兩個人或事物，比較常用的有兩種結構。

1. 肯定結構：as + 形容詞原級 + as，意思就是「和……一樣」。

Jimmy is as tall as his father.
吉米和他爸爸一樣高。

My hamburger is as big as yours.
我的漢堡和你的一樣大。

（yours 表示 your hamburger，這裡也複習p.45「物主代名詞」的用法）

2. 否定結構：not as + 形容詞原級 + as 或

not so + 形容詞原級 + as，意思就是「沒有……那麼……」。

This dish is not as delicious as that one.
這盤菜沒有那盤菜好吃。

My score is not so good as his.
我的成績沒有他的那麼好。

2. 形容詞的比較級

形容詞的比較級用於兩個人或事物的比較，結構為「形容詞比較級+ than」，意就是「比……更……」。

Tom is taller than Jim.
湯姆比吉姆高。

This picture is more beautiful than that one.
這張畫比那張畫漂亮。

3. 形容詞的最高級

形容詞的最高級用於三個或三個以上的人或事物的比較，結構為：「the + 形容詞最高級 + 比較範圍」，意思就是「最……」。

This is the most important part of this book.
這是這本書最重要的部分。

Peter is the youngest basketball player in the school.
彼得是這所學校年齡最小的籃球運動員。

要注意喔！

當句子中使用形容詞最高級時，形容詞前面一定要加 **the**，句中通常要加上「限定範圍」的短語。如：

Paul is the best student in his class.
保羅是班上最好的學生。

在這裡，**in his class**「在他班上」就是限定了一個範圍，說保羅是在這個範圍中最好的學生。

1. 在下面這封信裡面的形容詞下面劃線吧！。

<u>Dear</u> Ann,

I'm so happy! It's Christmas today. It's cold outside, windy and dry, but in my clean little room it's warm. My brother Ken bought a nice Christmas tree. We decorated（裝飾）it and it looks very beautiful.

Twenty people are here, in our big house. They are all my parents' friends. It's noisy but I like it. Ken and I have got so many presents, and mine is really a big one. And there's something special in the red box, but it's for Susan, my sister.

Tomorrow we're going to ski at Blue Mountain. How wonderful! Mom is calling me for dinner, and I have to stop here.

Best wishes,

Dorothy

2. 寫出下列單字的反義詞。

例 **good** __bad__

1. sad _____   2. thin _____   3.hot _____   4. dangerous _____

5. full _____   6. near _____   7. wet _____   8. hard _____

9. large _____   10. early _____   11.short _____   12.strong _____

3. 根據中文提示，把這些單字重組，完成句子。要注意句中形容詞的位置喔！

例 這件雨衣是濕的。

wet, raincoat, is, this

This raincoat is wet.

1. 這是個空瓶子。

   is, bottle, this, an, empty

   _____.

2. 這些花是紅色的。

   red, the, are, flowers

   _____.

3. 絲綢摸起來很柔軟。

   the, feel, soft, silk

   _____.

4. 這部電腦出了一些問題。

   computer, with, there, wrong, the, is, something

   _____.

4. 寫出下列形容詞的比較級和最高級。

形容詞原級	比較級	最高級
late	later	latest
beautiful		
few		
important		
useful		

many		
far		
clean		
clever		
happy		
big		

5. 下列每個句子裡面都有一個地方不對，請把錯誤的地方畫出來，並在句子最後的括號裡面改正。

例 **This apple is much <u>big</u> than that one.** 　　　　**(bigger)**
　　這個蘋果比那個大的多。

1. Tony is tallest than Lily. 　　　　　　　　　　　(　　　　　　)

2. Who is the beautifulest girl in our school? 　　　(　　　　　　)

3. She is as cleverer as I. 　　　　　　　　　　　(　　　　　　)

4. Alice's hair is longer as Susan's . 　　　　　　　(　　　　　　)

5. Look! Kate is the faster runner of the three. 　　(　　　　　　)

6. Linda's box is heaviest of the three. Let's help her. 　(　　　　　　)

你做對了嗎？

1.

Dear Ann,

I'm so <u>happy</u>! It's Christmas today. It's <u>cold</u> outside, <u>windy</u> and <u>dry</u>, but in my <u>clean</u> <u>little</u> room it's <u>warm</u>. My brother Ken bought a <u>nice</u> Christmas tree. We decorated（裝飾）it and it looks very <u>beautiful</u>.

Twenty people are here, in our <u>big</u> house. They are all my parents' friends. It's <u>noisy</u> but I like it. Ken and I have got so <u>many</u> presents, and mine is really a <u>big</u> one. And there's something <u>special</u> in the <u>red</u> box, but it's for Susan, my sister.

Tomorrow we're going to ski at Blue Mountain. How <u>wonderful</u>! Mom is calling me for dinner, and I have to stop here.

Best wishes,

Dorothy

2.	1. happy	2. fat / thick	3. cold	4. safe
	5. empty	6. far	7. dry	8. easy / soft
	9. small	10. late	11. long / tall	12. weak

3.	1. This is an empty bottle.
	2. The flowers are red.
	3. The silk feels soft. （這裡注意動詞 feel 要變成第三人稱單數形式。）
	4. There is something wrong with the computer.

4.

形容詞原級	比較級	最高級
late	later	latest
beautiful	more beautiful	most beautiful
few	fewer	fewest
important	more important	most important
useful	more useful	most useful
many	more	most
far	farther / further	farthest / furthest
clean	cleaner	cleanest
clever	cleverer	cleverest
happy	happier	happiest
big	bigger	biggest

5.

1. tallest→taller （東尼比麗麗高。）

2. beautifulest→most beautiful
   （誰是我們學校裡面最漂亮的女生？）

3. cleverer→clever （她和我一樣聰明。）

4. as→than （愛麗絲的頭髮比蘇珊的長。）

5. faster→fastest （看！凱特是三個人當中跑得最快的。）

6. heaviest 前加 the
   （琳達的箱子是三個裡面最重的。我們幫幫她吧！）

♥ 確實了解每一題後，再進行下一章喔！

Unit 5.
副詞

Unit 5. 副詞

1. 什麼是副詞？

副詞是用來修飾動詞、形容詞、副詞（副詞可修飾副詞本身）或整個句子的詞，表示時間、地點、程度、方式等。如：

Carl runs fast.
卡爾跑得很快。（副詞fast修飾動詞run）

It is raining heavily outside.
外面雨下得很大。（副詞heavily修飾動詞rain）

These candies are very delicious.
這些糖果很好吃。（副詞very修飾形容詞delicious）

I can't walk too quickly.
我不能走得太快。（副詞too修飾副詞quickly）

Luckily, Mrs. Black won the lottery.
幸運的是，布萊克夫人中了彩票。（副詞luckily修飾全句）

2. 副詞的種類

副詞根據它們的意義，分成下面幾類：

時間副詞：主要表示「什麼時候」、「經常與否」。如：

always 總是	sometimes 有時	now 現在
then 那時	yesterday 昨天	at first 首先

地點副詞：包括表示地點的副詞和表示位置關係的副詞。如：

here 這裡	there 那裡	up 向上
down 向下	back 向後	everywhere 每個地方

程度副詞：主要表示程度的深淺。如：

much 很；非常	little 很少	very 非常
too 太	enough 足夠	quite 完全；十分

方式副詞：主要表示「怎樣地」。如：

quickly 快地	suddenly 突然地	warmly 熱情地
neatly 整潔地	quietly 安靜地	badly 糟糕地

疑問副詞：主要用來引導一個特殊問句。如：

how 如何	when 什麼時候
where 哪裡	why 為什麼

3. 副詞的位置

1. 副詞修飾動詞（包括動名詞和分詞）時，通常位於被修飾動詞的後面。如：

She is working hard.
她正在努力工作。（副詞hard修飾動詞working）

The old man walked slowly.
這位老人走得很慢。（副詞slowly修飾動詞walked）

2. 副詞修飾形容詞時，通常放在該形容詞的前面。如：

The boy is too young. He can't carry the heavy box.
這個男孩太小。他搬不動這個重箱子。（副詞too修飾形容詞young）

He is a very funny boy.
他是一個非常有趣的男孩。（副詞very修飾形容詞funny）

3. 副詞修飾其他副詞時，通常放在被修飾副詞的前面。如：

The girl dances very well.
這個女孩舞跳得非常好。（副詞very修飾副詞well）

4. 副詞修飾數字時，通常放在被修飾數字的前面。如：

Her grandpa is over eighty, but he is healthy.
她的爺爺八十多歲了，但還是很健康。（副詞over修飾數字eighty）

4. 副詞的排列順序

1. 副詞表示時間、地點時，小單位在前，大單位在後。如：

He comes from New York, America.
他來自美國紐約。
（New York是America裡的一個城市，New York比較小，所以放前面）

2. 副詞表示方式時，拼寫短的在前，拼寫長的在後，並用**and**或**but**等連接詞連接。如：

Please write slowly and carefully.
請寫慢一點、仔細一點。

3. 多個不同副詞排列，通常依此順序：程度+方式+地點+時間。如：

The man runs very slowly along the river at 6:30 every morning.
　　　　　　　　跑的程度　　　　地點　　　小時間　　　大的時間
這個人每天早晨六點半，都會沿著河邊慢跑。

⑤. 副詞的比較等級

　　副詞和形容詞一樣，也有三個比較等級：原級、比較級和最高級。

1. 表示「等於」時，用原級。如：

She runs as fast as I.
她跑得和我一樣快。

2. 表示二者比較時，用比較級。如：

She runs faster than I.
她跑得比我快。

3. 表示三者以上比較，意為「最……」時，用最高級。如：

She runs (the) fastest in the class.
她是班上跑得最快的。

要注意喔！

在上面副詞最高級的句型中，最高級前面的**the**通常可以省略。

6. 副詞比較級、最高級的構成

副詞比較等級的構成規則與形容詞大致相同。

1. 單音節詞／少數雙音節詞→比較級：原詞尾+ er
最高級：原詞尾+ est

原級	比較級	最高級
fast 快地	faster	fastest
late 晚地	later	latest
early 早地	earlier	earliest
near 近地	nearer	nearest
hard 辛苦地	harder	hardest

2. 兩個或兩個以上音節的詞→比較級：原詞前+ more
最高級：原詞前+ most

原級	比較級	最高級
quickly 快地	more quickly	most quickly
slowly 慢地	more slowly	most slowly
loudly 大聲地	more loudly	most loudly
quietly 安靜地	more quietly	most quietly
clearly 清楚地	more clearly	most clearly
carefully 細心地	more carefully	most carefully

3. 有些副詞的比較級和最高級的變化是不規則的，需特別記下來：

原級	比較級	最高級
well 好地	better	best
badly 壞地	worse	worst
much 大量地	more	most

far 遠地	farther/further	farthest/furthest
little 小地、少地	less	least

要注意喔！

early的結尾-ly並不是副詞結尾，它的比較級和最高級不用more或most構成，而是將y變為i，再加-er或-est，即earlier, earliest。這一點要特別記住。

7. 副詞比較等級的用法

副詞比較級和最高級用法與形容詞比較級和最高級用法大致相同。

1. 副詞的原級

副詞的原級比較用於兩個人或事物的比較，常用結構為：

1. 肯定結構：as + 副詞原級 + as，意為「和……一樣」

My father gets up as early as my mother.
我爸爸和我媽媽一樣早起床。。

2. 否定結構：not...as/so + 副詞原級 + as，意為「不及……」。

My father does not get up as early as my mother.
我爸爸沒有我媽媽早起床。

2. 副詞的比較級

副詞的比較級用於兩個人或事物的比較，結構為「副詞比較級 + than」，

意為 「比……更……」。

Tom studies harder than Jimmy.
湯姆比吉米更努力學習。

She speaks English more fluently than I.
她英語說得比我流利。

He learned more quickly than the other students.
他學得比其他學生快。

3. 副詞的最高級

　　副詞最高級用於三個或三個以上的人或事物的比較，結構為「the+副詞最高級+比較範圍」，意為「最……」。

Who sings (the) best in our class?
我們班誰唱歌唱得最好？

He likes the book (the) most.
他最喜歡這本書。

---

1. 幫下列副詞分類，填寫在相應的橫線上。

often	there	loudly	then	why	too
down	yesterday	where	enough	slowly	when
quite	everywhere	heavily	now		

1. 時間副詞：often _____

2. 地點副詞：_____

3. 方式副詞：_____

4. 程度副詞：_____

5. 疑問副詞：_____

2. 請填入適合的副詞。

例 **Jack was hungry. He ate his dinner <u>hungrily</u>.**
傑克很餓。他狼吞虎嚥地吃著晚餐。

1. I am a good basketball player. I play _____.

2. Dad was angry with me. He shouted at me _____.

3. Mr. Baker is a careful driver. He drives _____.

4. Ann is a fast swimmer. She swims _____.

5. The firemen were brave. They fought the fire _____.

3. 從方框中選擇最適當的副詞，並用其正確形式填空，每個詞只能用一次。

often	sweet	fast	good	late
too	how	outside	suddenly	

例 I **often** go to school by bus.
我經常搭公車上學。

1. Kate sings _____.

2. Lucy runs as _____ as her sister.

3. The man is too old to walk _____.

4. Tom woke up late this morning; he was the _____ to arrive.

5. The children are playing games _____.

6. Henry is _____ young to drive a car.

7. — _____ do you like the dishes?

   — Very much.

8. The driver braked _____ when he saw a dog ahead.

4. 寫出下列副詞的比較級和最高級。

副詞原級	比較級	最高級
late	later	latest
carefully		
quickly		
well		
much		
early		
clearly		
slowly		
loudly		
safely		
quietly		

5. 根據中文提示完成句子。

例 **Mary runs as   fast as me.**
瑪麗跑的和我一樣快。

1. She gets up ＿＿＿＿＿ ＿＿＿＿＿ ＿＿＿＿＿ her sister.

   她和姐姐起得一樣早。

2. Amy ＿＿＿＿＿ ＿＿＿＿＿ ＿＿＿＿＿ dancer, she dances ＿＿＿＿＿
   ＿＿＿＿＿ .

   艾咪是位優秀的舞者，她舞跳得很好。

3. The box ＿＿＿＿＿ ＿＿＿＿＿ ＿＿＿＿＿, little Tom ＿＿＿＿＿
   ＿＿＿＿＿ ＿＿＿＿＿ ＿＿＿＿＿.

   這個盒子太重了，小湯姆不太容易搬動它。

4. Which one do you like _____ _____ all the three?

這三個之中你最喜歡哪一個？

5. They _____ _____ _____ _____ _____ _____ _____ _____ _____.

他們每天下午四點鐘打籃球。

6. He was born _____ _____ _____ _____ _____ _____.

他出生在倫敦附近的一個小鎮。

你做對了嗎？

1.
1. then, yesterday, now

2. there, down, everywhere

3. loudly, slowly, heavily

4. too, enough, quite

5. why, where, when

2.
1. well（我是個籃球好手。我籃球打得不錯。）

2. angrily（爸爸對我很生氣。他生氣地對我大吼。）

3. carefully（貝克先生是個小心的司機。他開車很小心。）

4. fast（安是個很快的游泳者。她游泳游得很快。）

5. bravely（消防隊員很勇敢。他們勇敢地滅火。）

3.
1. sweetly（凱特歌唱得好。）

2. fast（露西和她姐姐跑得一樣快。）

3. well（這個人太老了走不太動。）

4. latest（湯姆今天早上起得很晚，他是最晚一個到的。）

5. outside（孩子們正在外面玩遊戲。）

6. too（亨利年齡太小，還不能開車。）

7. How（你覺得這些菜肴怎麼樣？非常喜歡。）

8. suddenly（司機看到前方有隻狗，突然地煞車。）

4.

副詞原級	比較級	最高級
late	later	latest
carefully	more carefully	most carefully
quickly	more quickly	most quickly
well	better	best
much	more	most
early	earlier	earliest
clearly	more clearly	most clearly
slowly	more slowly	most slowly
loudly	more loudly	most loudly
safely	more safely	most safely
quietly	more quietly	most quietly

5.

1. as early as
2. is a good; very well
3. is too heavy; cannot move it easily
4. best of
5. play basketball at four o'clock in the afternoon every day
6. in a small town near London

♥ 確實了解每一題後，再進行下一章喔！

Unit 6.
数量詞

Unit 6. 數量詞

1. 讓我們來認識數量詞

數量詞是表示數目多少或順序先後的詞，可以分為基數詞和序數詞。例如：

I have two sisters.
我有兩個姐妹。 （two 是基數詞）

Sunday is the first day of a week.
星期天是一星期的第一天。 （first 是序數詞）

2. 基數詞

表示數目多少**的數詞叫做基數詞**，如 one、two、three。用這些基數詞可以構成各式各樣的數字。為了讓大家更容易記住，我們將基數詞分為以下五類：

表示 1～12 的基數詞

1：one	2：two	3：three
4：four	5：five	6：six
7：seven	8：eight	9：nine
10：ten	11：eleven	12：twelve

表示 13～19 的基數詞

這七個詞都以-teen 結尾。

13：thirteen	14：fourteen
15：fifteen	16：sixteen
17：seventeen	18：eighteen
19：nineteen	

表示 20～99 的基數詞

1. 表示「幾十」（十的倍數）的數詞

這些能被十除盡的數詞都以–ty 結尾。

20：twenty	30：thirty
40：forty	50：fifty
60：sixty	70：seventy
80：eighty	90：ninety

※特別注意：

14	fourteen	19	nineteen
40	forty	90	ninety

2. 其他的兩位數數字

結尾不是零的兩位數數字，這些數詞的兩個位數中間用「-」來連接。例如：

21：twenty-one
53：fifty-three
75：seventy-five
98：ninety-eight

表示 100～999 的基數詞

1. 表示「幾百」（一百的倍數）的數詞

這種結尾是「00」的三位數數詞由 1～9 加上 hundred構成。例如：

100：a (one) hundred
200：two hundred
500：five hundred

2. 其他的三位數數字

不能被一百除盡的這些數字，百位數和十位數之間用 and 連接，十位數和個位數之間用「-」連接。例如：

> 101：one hundred and one
> 310：three hundred and ten
> 524：five hundred and twenty-four

1000以上的大數字

千、萬、億等大的數字怎麼說？請看下面的例子：

1000（一千）：a (one) thousand

3000（三千）：three thousand

1,000,000（一百萬）：a (one) million

5,000,000（五百萬）：five million

1,000,000,000（十億）：a billion

2,000,000,000（二十億）：two billion

要注意喔！

1. **hundred**、**thousand**、**million**、**billion** 前面有具體的數字時，後面不能加「**s**」，例如說 **three hundreds** 就是錯誤的，該說 **three hundred**（三百）才對。

   五百 **five hundred (O)**　　　**five hundreds (X)**

   那麼什麼時候可以加「**s**」呢？只有在表示「大概的數字」時詞尾才需要加「**s**」。例如說數以百計、數以千計時，就可以說 **hundreds of**、**thousands of**。

2. 英文沒有表示「萬」的單字。他們的「萬」就是十個千，也就是 **ten thousand**。如果是超過一萬，例如四萬呢？那就是四十個千，要說 **forty thousand**。

3. 序數詞

　　表示順序、「第幾個」的數詞叫做序數詞，例如 first（第一）、second（第二）、third（第三）。為了讓大家更容易記住，我們也將序數詞分為以下三類：

表示 1～3 的序數詞

這三個序數詞跟別的序數詞長得都不一樣，需要背起來。

第一：first
第二：second
第三：third

表示 4～19 的序數詞

這16個序數詞是由「基數詞+ th」構成。

第4：fourth	第5：fifth	第6：sixth
第7：seventh	第8：eighth	第9：ninth
第10：tenth	第11：eleventh	第12：twelfth
第13：thirteenth	第14：fourteenth	第15：fifteenth
第16：sixteenth	第17：seventeenth	第18：eighteenth
第19：nineteenth		

※特別注意：

12	twelve	19	nineteen
第12	twelfth	第19	ninth

表示 20～100 的序數詞

1. 結尾是「0」（十的倍數）的序數詞

寫這種可以被十除盡的序數詞時，要把原本的基數詞的詞尾「y」改寫成「i」，然後加 -eth。例如 20 原本是 twenty，把它的 y 拿掉，換上 ieth，就會變成 twentieth（第二十）了。

第20：twentieth　　第30：thirtieth
第40：fortieth　　第50：fiftieth
第60：sixtieth　　第70：seventieth
第80：eightieth　　第90：ninetieth

100 也是「0」結尾，那麼它的序數詞怎麼說呢？「百」的序數詞是在 hundred 詞尾直接加 -th，其他 100 的倍數也一樣喔。例如：

第200：two hundredth
第500：five hundredth
第700：seven hundredth
第800：eight hundredth

2. 其他的兩位數序數詞

這些序數詞是由基數詞「幾十幾」變化而來的。寫這些數字時，十位數不變，個位數參考前面提到的 1～9 序數詞變化方式，然後十位數和個位數中間再用「-」連接。例如：

第21：twenty-first
第53：fifty-third
第84：eighty-fourth
第99：ninety-ninth

要注意喔！

1. 在**4～19**的序數詞中，有幾個序數詞不是簡單地把基數詞加上「**-th**」就可以解決的。現在我們把這些列出來，要注意它們怎麼拼喔！

fifth（第五）　　　　eighth（第八）

ninth（第九）　　　　twelfth（第十二）

2. 序數詞有縮寫形式，也就是在阿拉伯數字的後面加上序數詞的最後兩個字母。例如：

first：1st　　　second：2nd　　　third：3rd

fifth：5th　　　forty-first：41st　　　fifty-second：52nd

sixty-third：63rd

4. 分數、倍數、小數和百分數的表示

分數

分數的分子用基數詞表示，分母用序數詞表示。如果分子大於 1 時，分母要用序數詞的複數形式表示。例如：

1/3 one-third　　　　　　　2/3 two-thirds

1/4 one-fourth (one quarter)　　3/4 three-fourths

另外，1/4 也可以叫做 one quarter，而 1/2 則說 one half。

倍數

表示「兩倍」時比較特別，要用twice，而表示「三倍」及「三倍以上」的方式相同，用「基數詞 + times」的方式構成。例如：

Twice three is six.
二三得六。（3 的兩倍是 6。）

This room is three times the size of that one.
這個房間的面積是那個房間的三倍。

小數

　　小數點以前的數字用基數詞的讀法讀出；小數點以後的數，將每個數字一一讀出，而小數點讀作point。這和我們中文裡面，小數點之後的數字不會念「幾百幾十幾」，而是一個字一個字念出來一樣。例如：

1.6	one point six
0.6	zero point six
15.005	fifteen point zero zero five
0.006	zero point zero zero six

百分數

　　百分數中的百分號「%」讀作 percent。例如：

5%	five percent
0.5%	zero point five percent
96%	ninety-six percent

❺ 數詞的用法

年、月、日的表示方法

　　英文中表示日期的順序是：月／日／年（美式）或日／月／年（英式）。例如：

2012 年 12 月 1 日：December 1st, 2012（美式）或
　　　　　　　　　　1st December, 2012（英式）

　　知道了日期怎麼寫以後，來學一下它怎麼念吧！「月」直接念英語中表示月份的名詞，「日」念基數詞或序數詞都可以。例如：

5月7日 寫作：May 7(th)

　　　　讀作：May (the) seventh 或 May seven

10月1日寫作：October 1(st)

　　　　讀作：October (the) first 或 October one

（以上括弧內的部分可以省略不寫或不讀）

　　至於最麻煩的「年」應該怎麼念呢？你可以分成兩部分，先讀前面的兩位數，再讀後面的兩位數。例如：

1985年：nineteen eighty-five

1992年：nineteen ninety-two

要注意喔！

在年代中出現「零」的時候，讀法可能又不一樣。例如：

1806年：eighteen-o-six 或 eighteen six

1900年：nineteen hundred

2009年：two thousand and nine

時刻的表示法

1. 表示「整點」

　　說整點時，用一個基數詞就可以了。例如：

　　6:00：(at) six (o'clock) 或 (at) 6 (o'clock)

　　11:00：(at) eleven (o'clock) 或 (at) 11 (o'clock)

　　（以上括弧內的 o'clock 可以省略，也就是說「六點」可以直接說一個 six 就能表示了，很簡單吧！）

2. 表示「半點」

　　說半點（五點半、六點半等等）時，有兩個結構，一種是說「half past + 鐘

點數字」，一種是說「鐘點數 + thirty」。這樣講有點難懂吧？看幾個例子就很清楚了：

> 4:30： half past four 或 four thirty
>
> 6:30： half past six 或 six thirty
>
> （half 這個字就是「一半」的意思；past 有「超過、過了」的意思。）

3. 表示「幾點幾分」

說幾點幾分時，結構是鐘點數加上分鐘數。例如：

> 8:05：eight (o) five
>
> 8:50：eight fifty

4. 表示「幾點幾分」時，也可以用 past 和 to！

如果當時是「幾點半」之前，就用分鐘數 + past + 鐘點數，表示「幾點過了幾分」。例如：

> 10:20（10 點過 20 分）：twenty past ten
>
> 7:12（7 點過 12 分）：twelve past seven

而如果當時是「幾點半」以後，就用 60 分鐘減掉當時的分鐘數，加上 to 和下一個鐘點數，表示「還差幾分就幾點了」。例如：

> 8:50（差 10 分 9 點）：ten to nine
>
> 1:45（差15分2點）：a quarter to two 或 fifteen to two
>
> （記得 quarter 表示15分鐘。）

編號

編號在英語中可用序數詞或基數詞表示。用序數詞的話，要把它擺在名詞之前，並加定冠詞；基數詞則要放在名詞之後。書寫時，基數詞可以用阿拉伯數字表示。例如：

第九課：the ninth lesson 或 Lesson Nine

第三部分：the third part 或 Part Three

六號：Number 6（讀作 number six，縮寫為 No. 6）

第四行：Line 4（讀作line four）

　　那如果編號是很大的數字，尤其是三位數或三位數以上呢？這時候要讀就從左到右，把數字一個一個讀出來。例如：

302 號房：Room 302（讀作 room three-o-two）

第 2106 頁：Page 2106（讀作 page two-one-o-six）

貨幣的表示法

台幣的單位是 NT dollar。使用方法如下：

10 元：10 *NT dollars*

15 元：15 *NT dollars*

除了台幣，一些其他常用到的貨幣怎麼說呢？我們來看看美金與英鎊：

美國貨幣

美國貨幣的基本單位是 dollar，複數是 dollars，符號為 $。使用方法如下：

1 美元：1 dollar（US$1）

20 美元：20 dollars（US$20）

英國貨幣

英國貨幣的單位是 pound，複數是 pounds，符號為£。使用方法如下：

1 英鎊：1 pound（£1）

100 英鎊：100 pounds（£100）

1. 選出下列基數詞的正確寫法。

例 (A) 16   A. sixteen   B. sixty

1. (   ) 7   A. seventh   B. seven
2. (   ) 10   A. ten   B. tenth
3. (   ) 11   A. eleven   B. eleventh
4. (   ) 9   A. ninth   B. nine
5. (   ) 12   A. twelfth   B. twelve
6. (   ) 數以百計的 A. hundreds of   B. hundred of
7. (   ) 四千   A. four thousands B. four thousand
8. (   ) 四十億   A. four million   B. four billion

2. 寫出與下列基數詞對應的序數詞。

例 one   first

1. two _____   2. three _____   3. four _____

4. five _____   5. eight _____   6. nine _____

7. eleven _____   8. twelve _____   9. twenty _____

10. forty-one _____ 11. fifty-two _____   12. sixty-three _____

13. seventy-four _____ 14. eighty _____   15. ninety _____

3. 下列這些和數字有關的詞用英文該怎麼念呢？

例 1/3 one third

1. 20% _____   2. 6/9 _____   3. 0.7 _____

4. 20 倍 _____   5. 8:30 _____   6. 0.08 _____

7. 2007 年＿＿＿＿＿＿＿＿＿＿＿＿＿

8. 9 月 1 日＿＿＿＿＿＿＿＿＿＿＿＿

9. 5:30＿＿＿＿＿＿＿＿＿＿＿＿＿＿

10. 5:15＿＿＿＿＿＿＿＿＿＿＿＿＿

11. 第七課＿＿＿＿＿＿＿＿＿＿＿＿

12. 第1007 頁＿＿＿＿＿＿＿＿＿＿＿

4. 根據中文提示，寫出它們的英文翻譯吧！

例 二加二等於四。

Two and two is four.

1. 2012年2月5日。

＿＿＿＿＿＿＿＿＿＿＿＿＿＿＿.

2. 4×4=16。

＿＿＿＿＿＿＿＿＿＿＿＿＿＿＿.

3. 5+6=11。

＿＿＿＿＿＿＿＿＿＿＿＿＿＿＿.

4. 這個箱子的重量是那個箱子的三倍。

＿＿＿＿＿＿＿＿＿＿＿＿＿＿＿.

5. 這條河的寬度是那條河的四倍。

＿＿＿＿＿＿＿＿＿＿＿＿＿＿＿.

你做對了嗎？

| 1. | 1. B | 2. A | 3. A | 4. B | 5. B | 6. A | 7. B | 8. B |

2.	1. second	2. third	3. fourth
	4. fifth	5. eighth	6. ninth
	7. eleventh	8. twelfth	9. twentieth
	10.forty-first	11.fifty-second	12. sixty-third
	13. seventy-fourth	14. eightieth	15. ninetieth

3.	1. twenty percent
	2. six-ninths
	3. zero point seven
	4. twenty times
	5. half past eight
	6. zero point zero eight
	7. (the year) two thousand and seven
	8. September (the) first 或 September one
	9. half past five 或 five thirty
	10. a quarter past five 或 fifteen past five 或 five fifteen
	11. the seventh lesson 或 Lesson Seven
	12.page one o o seven

4.

1. February 5th, 2012

2. Four times four is sixteen.

3. Five plus six is eleven.

4. This box is three times the weight of that box.

5. This river is four times the width of that river.

 確實了解每一題後，再進行下一章喔！

數量詞是很重要的觀念，基數詞、序數詞一定要分清楚，記得多複習幾次喔！

Unit 7.
介系詞

Unit 7. 介系詞

1. 什麼是介系詞？

　　介系詞通常是用來表示句子中各個詞之間的關係，尤其常用在名詞、代名詞、有名詞作用的短語前面。它們每個都長得不太一樣，看起來很難懂，所以在這一章可要多努力把它們的使用方法背起來喔！

It's about nine o'clock now.
現在大概是九點鐘。
（介系詞 about 用來表明後面的時間「大概」是什麼時候）

There is a kite in the sky.
天上有一個風箏。
（介系詞 in 用來表示 kite 與 sky 的關係，也就是風箏在天空「中」）

Julia will have a party on Sunday.
星期天茱莉亞將會辦一個派對。
（介系詞 on 表示 party 和 Sunday 的關係，也就是派對「在」禮拜天辦）

Helen is like her mom.
海倫像她媽媽。
（介系詞 like 表示「像」的意思）

2. 時間介系詞

　　時間介系詞就是表示時間的介系詞。英文中最常見的時間介系詞有 at、in、on、before、after 和 from。

at、in 和 on

　　這三個詞都表示時間。其中 at 主要指具體的鐘點（講「幾點鐘」時使用）；in 一般指某一段時間「之內」；on 指「在某一天」。

➡ at

1. 表示具體的時刻：意思是「在某一時刻」，常跟 o'clock、half past six 等表示具體時間的短語用在一起。例如：

He always gets up at seven every morning.
他每天早上都在七點起床。

The sports meet will begin at 9:30.
運動會在九點半開始。

2. **表示人的年齡**：習慣用語 at the age of 意思是「在……歲時」，常用在一般過去式中。例如：

The poor little girl died at the age of eleven.
那個可憐的小女孩在 11 歲的時候就死了。

I was in junior high school when I was at the age of 13.
我 13 歲的時候在上國中。

3. **表示一段時間**：意思是「在……的這段期間」。例如：

It is very cold at night.
晚上非常寒冷。

Susan and her family had a good time at Christmas.
蘇珊和家人在聖誕節那一段時間過得很開心。
（這裡不是只指在耶誕節當天，還包含聖誕節附近那整段時間。）

 in

　　in 用來表示一段時間，常與 January、February 等表示月份的詞和 spring、summer 等表示季節的詞連在一起用，也常會用在習慣用語中。例如：

Flowers blossom in spring.
春天花會開。

You shouldn't be sleeping in the morning.
你不應該在早上睡覺。

 on

　　on 表示具體的某一天，意思是「在……那天」，常與 day 和表示星期幾或某個節日的詞一起用。例如：

We have seven classes on Monday.
我們星期一有七堂課。

Jane was born on a cold day.
珍在很冷的一天出生。

before 和 after

　　before和after這兩個詞用來表示時間的先後順序，説的是「在某件事、某個時間之前或之後」。

→ before

before 表示「在某個時間之前」。例如：

Lisa got everything ready before cooking.
麗莎在做飯之前把所有東西都準備好了。

We have to finish the work before Thursday.
我們必須在星期四之前把工作做完。

→ after

after 表示「在某個時間之後」。例如：

The boys often play football after school.
那些男生常常在放學後踢足球。

We sometimes take a walk after supper.
我們有時會在吃完晚餐後去散步。

from

from 的意思是「從……」，不只用在時間上，也可以拿來用在很多其他地方。這裡先介紹它當作時間介詞時的用法：它有「從……這個時候開始」的意思，常和介系詞 to 連用，組成「from... to...」的結構，意思是「從……這個時候到……那個時候」。例如：

We have classes from Monday to Friday.
我們從星期一到星期五都要上課。

She worked in the garden from the morning to the evening.
她在花園裡從早忙到晚。

要注意喔！

「from... to...」的結構也可以用來表示地點，意思也還是「從……到……」，只是講的是從某個地方到另一個地方，而不是從一個時間到另一個時間。例如：

This train goes from Beijing to Tianjin.
這班火車從北京到天津。

It takes me 10 minutes to walk from the school to my home.
我從學校走到家要花10分鐘。

❸ 方位介系詞

方位介系詞，也就是表示位置和地點的介系詞。最常見的方位介系詞有on、in、at、under 和 behind等。根據所表示方位的不同，它們可以分為以下幾類：

on、over 和 above

介系詞 on、over 和 above 都有「在某個東西上面」的意思。但雖然都是在上面，這三個詞的用法還是不一樣喔！有哪些不一樣呢？

➔ on

說 on 的話表示一個物體在另一個物體上面，而且兩個物體的表面是互相有接觸的。例如：

There is a lamp on the desk.
書桌上有一盞燈。
（燈不可能飄浮在桌子上方，一定和桌子有接觸）

An apple is on the ground.
有一顆蘋果在地上。
（蘋果也不可能飄著，一定是貼著地面）

on

➔ over

說 over 的話，表示一個東西在另一個東西上面，但兩個物體表面互相沒有碰到。例如：

A lamp hung over the table.
桌子上方掛著一盞燈。
（燈是掛著的，和桌面沒有接觸）

There is a colourful lantern over the baby's cradle.
嬰兒搖籃的上方有一個彩色的燈籠。
（燈籠也是掛著的，和搖籃沒有接觸）

over

➔ above

 表示兩個物體一個在另一個的上方，但不一定是在正上方，而且兩個物體之間也沒有接觸。例如：

The plane is flying above the clouds.
飛機在雲層上飛行。

Look! A lot of birds are flying above the trees.
看！好多鳥在樹的上空飛。

above

under 和 below

under 和 below 都有「在……下面」的意思，不過雖然都是在下面，這兩個詞也是有區別的。差別在哪呢？

➡ under

under 表示一個東西在另一個東西的正下方。例如：

There is a cat under the table.
桌子下面有一隻貓。

The river runs under the bridge.
河水從橋下流過。

under

➡ below

below 表示一個東西在另一個的下面，但不強調是在正下方。例如：

Our classroom is below theirs.
我們的教室位置比他們教室低。

Jane dived below the surface of the water.
珍妮潛到了水面下。

below

in

in 表示位置「在某個東西的裡面」，也可以用來表示「在一個很大的範圍內」。例如：

Lucy found a wardrobe in the room.
露西在房間裡發現一個衣櫥。

There are some books in the box.
箱子裡面有幾本書。

A group of tourists have arrived in Paris.
旅行團已經到達了巴黎。

We saw the animal show in the zoo.
我們在動物園裡看了動物表演。

in

at、about 和 around

這三個介系詞的意思有點像，at 表示「在某個地點」，about 和 around則表示位置「在某個東西周圍一帶」。它們應該怎麼使用呢？

 at

at 表示位於某個地點。如：

The family is eating at a table.
那一家人正坐在桌子那裡吃飯。

I met Patrick at the railway station.
我在火車站遇到派崔克。

at

➡ about 和 around

about 和 around 這兩個詞都可以表示「在……周圍」，也有「把……圍繞起來」的意思。這兩個詞有時可以互相代換，例如：

There is a fence about / around the house.
房子周圍有一圈籬笆。

不過習慣上這兩個詞有時會有一些微妙的不同。about 有一種「到處散佈」的感覺，而較不是規則地、有系統地排好。請看以下的例子：

The children ran around the Christmas tree and sang happily.
孩子們繞著聖誕樹跑，高興地唱歌。

The children ran about the place and sang happily.
孩子們到處隨便亂跑，高興地唱歌。

about/around

behind

behind 表示位置「在某個東西的後面」。例如：

Eric sits behind me.
艾瑞克坐在我後面。

Sally hid herself behind a tree.
莎莉躲在樹後面。

behind

要注意喔！

behind 表示「在某個東西後面」，那如果是在前面呢？英文裡面沒有一個單字可以直接表達「在某個東西前面」的意思，而是用介系詞片語 **in front of** 來表示。例如：

There is an apple tree in front of the house.
房子前面有棵蘋果樹。

between

　　between 表示位置「在兩個東西之間」。例如：

The office building is between the swimming pool and the playground.
辦公大樓在游泳池和操場之間。

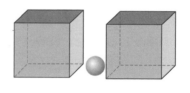

between

④. 表示移動方向的介系詞

　　在英文中，有一種介系詞表示的不是靜止不動的「位置」，而是一種動態的移動方式，有「朝著某個地方」、「向著某個地方」的意思。最常見的動向介系詞有 into、out of、up、down、from、to、through 和 along，在這裡我們一個一個介紹。

into 和 out of

　　這兩個字都是朝著某個方向移動的意思。那麼它們表示的方向有什麼不一樣呢？

➡ into

　　into 表示「從外面向裡面移動」的意思。例如：

John jumped into the swimming pool.
約翰跳進了游泳池。

I put the books into a large bag.
我把書放進一個大袋子裡。

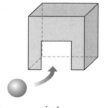

into

➔ out of

out of 是一個介系詞片語,表示「從裡面向外面移動」的意思。例如:

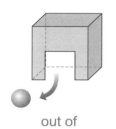

out of

We looked out of the window and saw many flowers.
我們向窗外看,看到很多花。

She took the present out of the box.
她把禮物從盒子裡拿出來。

up 和 down

up 和 down 這兩個詞和前面表示「裡外」的方向不同,表達的是「上下」的方向。它們有什麼差別呢?

➔ up

up 表示「由下面向上面移動」,常與 climb 等和上下移動有關的動詞用在一起。例如:

The monkey climbed up the tree quickly.
猴子很快地爬到樹上去了。

I opened the door and went up the stairs.
我打開門,上樓去了。

up

➔ down

down 表示「由上到下」或「沿著某個東西向下移動」。例如:

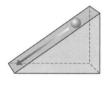

A ball rolled down the slope.
一顆球沿著坡滾下去了。

Tears poured down her face.
淚水從她的臉上流下。

down

from 和 to

有了進出、上下,當然還要有表達「來去」的介系詞。它們就是 from 和 to,from表示起點,to 表示終點。

from

from 表示「從……」、「來自……」。如：

He is from a coastal city in Sweden.
他來自瑞典的一個沿海城市。

I've got a birthday present from Joe.
我收到了喬送給我的生日禮物。

from

to

to 的意思是「到某個地方」、「向某個方向」，和 from 剛好相反。在它前面最常出現的動詞就是 go。例如：

Let's go to school.
我們去上學吧。

She went to Yellowstone National Park last Sunday.
她上星期天去了黃石國家公園。

to

across、through 和 along

across、through 和 along 這三個介詞都有「經過」的意思，但它們的用法都不一樣喔！有哪些差別呢？這些光用文字可能有點難理解，你可以看看插圖，會更清楚喔！

across

across 表示人或物從一個平面上面經過，有「橫著穿過去、從上面穿過去」的意思，常與 street（馬路），bridge（橋）等需要「過」的名詞用在一起。例如：

There is a stone bridge across the river.
有一座石橋橫跨河的兩岸。

Go across the street, and you'll find a stationery shop.
過馬路以後，你會發現一家文具店。

across

→ through

through 表示「從某個東西的裡面穿過去」。例如：

We walked through the woods.
我們穿過樹林。

The needle pierced through the cloth.
針穿過了布。

through

→ along

along 表示「沿著……」的意思，常與 road（馬路）、street（街道）、river（河）等長長的、可以沿著它走的名詞用在一起。例如：

Dick and Wendy walked together along the river.
迪克和溫蒂一起沿著河邊走。

Go along the road, and then turn left.
沿著這條路走下去，然後向左轉。

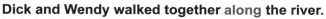

along

⑤ 表示方式、手段的介系詞

不只是時間和地點，表示一些事情的作法時，也可以用介系詞。最常見的「階段、手段」介系詞有 by、with 和 in。它們的用法有什麼不一樣呢？

by

by 表示「靠……來達到某個目的」、「用……來達到某個目的」。例如：

My mother goes to work by bus every day.
我媽媽每天坐公車上班。

Henry made a living by painting.
亨利以畫畫維生。

with

with 表示「使用……來做某件事」。例如：

We write with a pen.
我們用筆寫字。

He dug the ground with a shovel.
他用鏟子挖地。

要注意喔！

介系詞 **by** 和 **with** 雖然都有「靠……」、「用……」的意思，但 **by** 通常用在「達到比較抽象的目的」的時候，**with** 通常用在「做具體的事」的時候。

in

用來表達時間、位置的 in 也可以拿來表示手段喔！它是表達「用……語言」的意思。例如：

We talked in English.
我們用英文交談。

She can sing this song in French.
她會用法文唱這首歌。

❻ 其他介系詞的用法

for

1. 表示目的、對象，意思是「為了……」

Santa Claus said, "I have a gift for you."
聖誕老人說：「我有一個為了你準備的禮物。」

2. 表示原因，意思是「因為……」

Thank you for your dinner.
謝謝你請我吃晚餐。

I'm sorry for being late.
因為我遲到了，所以我很抱歉。

about

about 表示某種事物的內容，意思是「關於」。例如：

The movie is about a lion, a witch and a wardrobe.
這部電影是關於獅子、女巫和衣櫥的。

The book is about the history of Belgium.
這本書是講比利時的歷史。

with

1. 表示「和……一起」

Can you come with me?
你可以跟我一起來嗎？

Judy did chores with her sister.
茱蒂和她的姐姐一起做家事。

2. 表示「對於……」

Miss Wilson is very strict with her students.
威爾遜小姐對她的學生非常嚴格。

We are content with your answer.
我們對你的回答很滿意。

3. 表示人或物的性質或特點，意思是「帶著」、「帶有」。

The girl with red hair is Wendy's sister.
有紅頭髮的女孩是溫蒂的姐姐。

I saw a woman with sunglasses on the beach.
我在海灘上看到一個戴太陽眼鏡的女人。

in

in 表示「穿著……」。例如：

The boy in blue is my brother.
穿藍衣服的男孩是我的弟弟。

Who is that girl in red?
那個穿紅衣服的女孩是誰？

要注意喔！

1. 介系詞 **about** 既有「在……周圍」的意思，又有「關於」的意思，注意不要把這兩個意思搞混了。

2. 介系詞 **in** 可以表示時間、地點、穿著等，用法很廣泛，也不要搞混了喔！

of

of 表示所屬關係，意思是「屬於……的」。例如：

This is a map of the world.
這是一張世界地圖。

The boy is standing by the back door of the classroom.
男孩站在教室的後門旁。

like

like 有比較的意思，表示「像……」、「和……相似」。例如：

John is like his father.
約翰很像他的爸爸。

The lady looks like an actress.
這位小姐看起來像個演員。

要注意喔！

like 既可以當做介詞，也可以當做動詞，但是意思不一樣，在句子裡使用的位置也不一樣，使用的時候要小心喔！請看下面的例子：

Helen likes her mother.
海倫很喜歡她的媽媽。
（**like** 在這裡是動詞，前面沒有別的動詞）

Helen is like her mother.
海倫很像她的媽媽。
（**like** 在這裡是介系詞，前面要加動詞 **is**）

統整常見介系詞：

表示時間	at、in、on、before、after、from
表示方位	on、over、above、under、below、in、at、about、around、behind、between
表示移動方向	into、out of、up、down、from、to、across、through、along
表示方式、手段	by、with、in
表「目的、為了……」	for
表「關於」	about
表「和……一起」	with
表「關於」	about
穿著……（顏色）	in
表「屬於」	of

1. 選擇正確的介系詞，把對應的英文字母號填在每句話的括弧內。

例 The train leaves (C) 2:30 p.m.

火車在下午2:30發車。

1. I have an ache ( ) my arm.

2. The train is passing ( ) the tunnel.

3. Can you come to tea ( ) us ( ) Sunday?

4. Tom and Bill are twins. They look a lot ( ) each other.

5. Be careful when you walk ( ) the street.

6. The gardeners work in the garden ( ) Monday ( ) Friday.

7. Many people are waiting ( ) the bus ( ) the bus stop.

8. How did they come here? Mm, ( ) airplane.

A. by	B. on	C. at	D. for	E. in	F. to
G. like	H. with	I. through	J. from	K. across	

2. 從 A、B、C三個選項中，選擇最符合題意的一項。

例 School usually starts _A_ autumn.

A. in   B. on   C. at

學校通常在秋天開學。

1. The bus arrived _____ 7:30 a.m.

   A. on   B. at   C. in

2. Five is the number _____ four and six.

   A. at   B. among   C. between

3. The story is _____ a beauty and a beast.

   A. about   B. around   C. for

4. Your mouth is _____ your nose.

   A. under   B. below   C. near

5. We'll have an English party _____ the end of this term.

   A. in   B. at   C. on

6. Eric went _____ the cinema last night. He saw a film there.

   A. from   B. to   C. into

7. Did you go to the zoo _____ foot?

   A. by   B. on   C. with

8. Birds fly _____ wings.

   A. by   B. with   C. in

1.

1. E（我的手臂很痛。）

2. I（火車正在通過隧道。）

3. H；B（你禮拜天可以過來和我們一起喝茶嗎？）

4. G（湯姆和比爾是雙胞胎。他們長得很像。）

5. K（過馬路時要小心。）

6. J；F（園丁們禮拜一到禮拜五在花園裡工作。）

7. D；C（很多人在公車站等公車。）

8. A（他們怎麼來這裡的？嗯，坐飛機。）

2.

1. B（公車在早上七點半來了。）

2. C（五是介於四和六之間的那個數字。）

3. A（這是個關於美女和野獸的故事。）

4. B（嘴巴長在鼻子下面。）

5. B（我們這學期末會舉行一個英文晚會。）

6. B（艾瑞克昨天晚上去電影院，在那裡看了一場電影。）

7. B（你們是用走的去動物園嗎？）

8. B（鳥用翅膀飛。）

♥ 確實了解每一題後，再進行下一章喔！

Unit 8.
連接詞

Unit 8. 連接詞

1. 讓我們來認識連接詞

連接詞是連接單詞、短語或句子的一種詞。顧名思義就是用來連接其他東西，不能獨立當做句子的一個成分。

2. 常見連接詞的基本用法

and

and 表示並列、對稱，是「和」的意思。例如：

They began to sing and dance.
他們開始唱唱跳跳。

I like basketball, football and table tennis.
我喜歡籃球、足球和乒乓球。

both... and...

把 both 和 and 放在一起，就是加強 and 的語氣，表示「這個人或物和那個人或物兩個都⋯⋯」的意思。例如：

Both you and he are interested in computers.
你和他兩人都對電腦感興趣。

They can speak both English and French.
他們既會講英文，也會講法文。

not only... but (also)...

這個用法表示把兩件事、物並列，有「不但⋯⋯而且還⋯⋯」的意思。例如：

Jenny can play not only basketball but also volleyball.
珍妮不但會打籃球，而且還會打排球。

Not only you but also Jim often comes late.
不光是你，吉姆也常遲到。

neither... nor...

　　這個也是把兩件事、物並列的用法，但和 not only... but also... 不同的是，它們代表的是「這個人事物和那個人事物兩個都不……」的意思，是否定的。例如：

Neither you nor he is late for class.
你和他上課都沒遲到。

Neither you nor I am right.
你不對，我也不對。

or

　　or 就是「或」的意思，有兩個以上的選項時使用。例如：

Is it big or small?
它是大的還是小的？

Do you come to school by bike or by bus?
你是腳踏車還是搭公車來上學？

要注意喔！

在並列講兩件事時，**or** 通常用於否定語氣的句子，**and** 用於肯定語氣的句子。例如：

I don't like coffee or tea.
我既不喜歡喝咖啡，也不喜歡喝茶。

I like coffee and tea.
我喜歡喝咖啡和茶。

either... or...

　　這個組合也是表示有兩個以上的選項，有「選這個，不然就是那個」的意思。例如：

Either you or I have to do the housework.
你得做家事，不然就我做。

You may either stay here or go with us.
你可以待在這裡，不然就跟我們去。

but

but 就是「但是」的意思，表示轉折的語氣。例如：

I like the style of the dress, but I don't like the color.
我喜歡這衣服的款式，但我不喜歡它的顏色。

The skirt is nice, but it's too expensive.
這條裙子很不錯，但是太貴了。

for

for 是「因為」的意思，在講原因的時候用。例如：

They must be at home now, for it's raining.
他們現在一定在家，因為正在下雨。

He is absent today, for he is ill.
他今天沒來，因為他生病了。

because

because 也是表示原因的連接詞，是「因為」的意思，和 for 可以替換著使用。例如：

John didn't come to school yesterday because he was ill.
約翰昨天沒來上學，因為他生病了。

They were sad because they lost the match.
他們因為比賽輸了，所以很沮喪。

要注意喔！

我們中文常常說「因為……所以……」，但在英文中 **because / for**（因為）和 **so**（所以）卻不能夠用在同一個句子中，要單獨使用。請看下面的例子：

因為媽媽給她買了一頂漂亮的帽子，所以她非常高興。

She was very happy because her Mom bought her a beautiful hat. (O)

Her Mom bought her a beautiful hat, so she was very happy. (O)

Because her Mom bought her a beautiful hat, so she was very happy. (X)

so

so 也是和原因有關的連接詞，但它代表的是「所以」的意思。例如：

My sister is waiting for me, so I must be off now.
我姐姐在等我，所以我得走了。

He got up late, so he missed the bus.
他太晚起來了，所以錯過了公車。

when

when 是和時間有關的連接詞，意思是「當……的時候」。例如：

Please come visit me when you are free.
有空的時候請來拜訪我。

Laura was cooking when the power went out.
停電的時候，蘿拉正在做飯。

after

after 是在說事情發生的先後順序時用的，意思是「在……之後」。例如：

I will invite all of you to dinner after my house is completed.
房子蓋好以後，我會請你們大家吃飯。

Melanie went to bed soon after it got dark.
梅蘭妮天黑以後，過了不久就上床睡覺了。

before

和 after 相反，before 講的是「在……之前」的意思。例如：

You must clean the room before you leave.
你在走之前要先把房間收乾淨。

The little pig ran away before the wolf came.
小豬在狼來之前就先逃走了。

as soon as

as soon as 也是表示時間的連接詞，意思是「一……就……」。例如：

I'll call you as soon as I arrive.
我一到，就打電話給你。

You should go home as soon as it stops raining.
雨一停，你就應該趕快回家。

if

if 表示條件，是「如果」的意思。例如：

We will go to the zoo if it does not rain tomorrow.
如果明天不下雨，我們就去動物園。

If you have any questions, please let me know.
如果你有什麼問題，請告訴我。

although 和 though

although 和 though 的用法相同，都是「雖然」的意思。例如：

Although he has never been to America, he has some American friends.
雖然他沒去過美國，但他有一些美國朋友。

Mary has to play the piano every day though she doesn't like it.
雖然瑪麗不喜歡彈鋼琴，但她還是不得不天天彈。

要注意喔！

我們中文常常說「雖然……但是……」，可是在英文裡面的 **although** 和 **though** （雖然）和**but**（但是）卻不能用在同一個句子中喔。請看下面的例子：

雖然他很虛弱，但他還是盡力完成工作。

Although he was weak, but he tried his best to do the work. (X)

Although he was weak, he tried his best to do the work. (O)

He was weak, but he tried his best to do the work. (O)

1. 用 and, or 或 but 填空看看。

例 **I would like some bread and butter.**
我想要一點麵包和奶油。

1. Both Dad _____ Mom are teachers.

2. I don't like coffee _____ tea.

3. We bought a cake yesterday, _____ we didn't eat it.

4. Merry Christmas _____ Happy New Year!

5. Are you going there by train _____ by plane?

2. 下列每個句子中都有一個錯誤，在下面加上底線，並在句子後的括弧內改正吧！

例 **Both Tom and Jerry _is_ in Class Two. (are)**
湯姆和傑瑞都在二班。

1. You naughty kids! Neither Harry or Judy is to blame. (　)

2. Either boys and girls were chosen to give the performance. (　)

3. Both Jeff and Sheila likes flying kites. (　)

4. This cartoon is popular among not only children and also adults. (　)

3. 從三個選項中，選出最適合填到句子裡的選項。

例 **I would like some bread _____ butter. (A)**

A. and　　　　**B. but**　　　**C. nor**

我想要一點麵包和奶油。

1. The Greens were watching TV _____ the power went out.

   A. before　　　B. after　　　　C. when

2. You can play basketball with Ben _____ you finish your homework.

   A. before　　　B. after　　　　C. when

3. Maggie was dead tired. She went to bed _____ it got dark.

   A. before　　　B. after　　　　C. when

4. _____ it is raining, the match is still going on.

   A. Because　　B. Although　　C. But

5. Just let me know _____ you need any help.

   A. because　　B. before　　　C. if

6. The concert was great, _____ it could be better.

   A. but　　　　B. although　　C. or

你做對了嗎？

1.	1. and （我的父母都是老師。）
	2. or （茶或咖啡我都不喜歡。）
	3. but （我們昨天買了一塊蛋糕，但是我們沒把它吃掉。）
	4. and （聖誕快樂，新年快樂！）
	5. or （你去那裡是坐火車還是飛機？）

2.	1. neither→either （你們這些頑皮的孩子！不是哈利的錯，就是茱蒂的錯。）
	2. Either→Both （男生和女生都被選中參加演出。）
	3. likes→like （傑夫和希拉都喜歡放風箏。）
	4. and→but （這卡通不但小孩很喜歡，成年人也喜歡。）

3.	1. C （停電的時候，格林一家正在看電視。）
	2. B （你功課寫完後，就可以和班去打籃球了。）
	3. A （梅姬累得要死，天還沒黑就上床睡覺了。）
	4. B （雖然在下雨，但是比賽仍在進行。）
	5. C （如果你需要幫忙，就告訴我。）
	6. B （那場音樂會超棒，雖然還可以更好啦。）

♥ 確實了解每一題後，再進行下一章喔！

Unit 9.
感嘆詞

Unit 9. 感嘆詞

1. 什麼是感嘆詞？

感嘆詞是用來表達喜、怒、哀、樂等感情或情緒的詞，因為是在激動時說出的，通常會很短，而且在講完這些詞之後，一般都會接驚嘆號「!」。接下來我們看看感嘆詞常見的用法大概有哪些吧！要注意的是，感嘆詞其實絕對不只下面列的這些，因為人表達情緒時會用到的語句實在太多了，數也數不完！

2. 常見感嘆詞的基本用法

歡呼時使用

Hurrah! 萬歲！太棒了！	Bravo! 萬歲！幹得好!
Yipee! 太好了！	There! 你看！

Hurrah! We won the game!
我們贏了！萬歲！

表示讚賞

Excellent! 好極了！太棒了！	Great! 太棒了！	Terrific! 太棒了！
Well done! 做得好！	Good! 很好！	

Excellent! You did a good job.
太好了！你做得很好。

表示驚奇

Oh! 啊！哇！喔！	**Good heavens!** 天啊！

Dear me! / Oh, dear! / Dear, dear!
天啊！

Good heavens! A fierce dog is running after me!
天啊！有一隻好兇的狗在追我！

表示哀傷

Oh! 噢！太糟了！
Alas! 慘了！（可以在較正式或有點年代的書中看到，一般人不太可能會説。）

Alas! I failed my maths exam again.
哎呀！我數學又考不及格了。

表示痛苦

Ouch!
哎喲！好痛！

Ouch! Be careful, you're stepping on my foot.
哎喲，好痛！小心點，你踩到我的腳了。

想引起別人注意時打招呼的聲音

Hey! 喂！嘿！	Hello! 哈囉！	Hi! 嗨！

Hi! How are you these days?
嗨！這些天還好嗎？

表示安慰

Here!
好了！沒事了！

Here! Don't cry!
好了，別哭了！

練習做做看

1. 根據圖畫內容，選擇適當的感嘆詞填空。

1 _____

2 _____

3 _____

4 _____

A. Hello!   B. Oh dear!   C. Shhh!   D. Goodbye!

參考解答

你做對了嗎？

| 1. D | 2. B | 3. A | 4. C |

♥ 確實了解每一題後，再進行下一章喔！

Unit 10.
動詞

Unit 10. 動詞

❶ 讓我們來認識動詞

表示一個「動作」或「狀態」的詞，就叫做動詞。表示動作的動詞很多，例如：

throw 投擲　　　walk 行走　　　dance 跳舞　　　sing 唱歌

表示狀態的動詞則例如：

be 是　　　have 有　　　smile 笑　　　cry 哭　　　sleep 睡覺

❷ 動詞的種類有哪些？

按照動詞的意思和在句子中的作用來劃分，動詞可以大略分成四種：

(實義動詞)

實義動詞也叫行為動詞，顧名思義就是和實際動作有關的動詞，是最普通的一種動詞。例如：

The lion opened its huge mouth and roared.
那頭獅子張開大嘴吼叫起來。

The earth orbits the sun.
地球繞著太陽轉。

Polar bears live in the North Pole.
北極熊生活在北極。

Elephants have long noses.
大象有長鼻子。

實義動詞又可分為**及物動詞**和**不及物動詞**兩類。

1. 及物動詞

及物動詞進行的動作是有對象的，這個動作一定是發生在什麼人、什麼東西身上。這種動詞的後面要接受詞。例如：

Judy found a Christmas gift in the stocking.
裘蒂在襪子裡找到了聖誕禮物。

We ate Sue's birthday cake.
我們吃了蘇的生日蛋糕。

2. 不及物動詞

　　不及物動詞不需要發生在什麼東西身上，就算沒有對象，一樣可以做這個動作，所以後面就不接受詞。例如：

The car stopped.
車停了。

The sun rises in the east.
太陽從東方升起。

連繫動詞

　　連繫動詞講的是一個人、一件事、或一個物品的狀態，必須和名詞、形容詞等一起使用。除了最基本的 be 動詞外，和感官有關的動詞也算是這一類。例如：

➡ be 動詞

I am from Hollywood.
我來自好萊塢。

The giant is very tall and strong.
巨人又高又壯。

Are you ready? Let's go.
你準備好了嗎？我們走吧。

Sally was late for school yesterday.
莎莉昨天上學遲到了。

➡ 感官動詞

　　常用的感官動詞有 look（看起來）、sound（聽起來）、feel（感覺到）、become（變成）、smell（聞起來）等。例如：

The boy looks very happy.
這個男孩看起來很高興。

The music sounds beautiful.
這音樂聽起來很美。

The silk feels very smooth.
絲綢摸起來很光滑。

The audience became excited.
觀眾變得激動起來。

The dish smells good.
這盤菜聞起來很香。

助動詞

助動詞就是「幫助其他動詞表達意思」的動詞，一定要和一個實義動詞一起用。助動詞有do、be動詞（is、am、are）、have、shall（should），will（would）等。它們和實義動詞一起構成各種時態，要表達否定和疑問等句子時也要靠它們。例如：

The child is crying.
那小孩在哭。
（小孩在哭是正在發生的事，助動詞 be 表示現在進行式。）

They will have a party on Sunday.
星期天他們會開一場派對。
（星期天還沒到，助動詞 will 表示未來式。）

Does he work in a hospital?
他是在醫院工作嗎？
（助動詞 do 幫助構成疑問句。）

Robert was punished by the teacher.
羅伯被老師處罰了。
（助動詞 be 幫助構成被動式。）

I don't know her telephone number.
我不知道她的電話號碼。
（助動詞 do 幫助構成否定結構）

情態動詞

這種動詞和說話的人的語氣、情緒有關。它不能單獨使用，一定要和原形動詞一起用。常見的情態動詞有shall、should、will、would、can、could、may、might、must、dare、need、ought to 等。例如：

The little boy can fly a kite.
這個小男孩會放風箏。

May I borrow your pen, Ann?
安，我可以借用妳的筆嗎？

I knew Martha would enjoy Disneyland.
我就知道瑪莎會喜歡迪士尼樂園。

Shall we meet at seven o'clock tomorrow?
我們要不要明天七點見？

❸ 動詞的原形、過去式和分詞形式

　　動詞有五種基本形式：動詞原形、第三人稱單數現在式、過去式、過去分詞、現在分詞。這五種形式的動詞和助動詞互相搭配，就可以構成不同的動詞時態和語氣。

1. 動詞原形

　　動詞原形就是沒有經過任何變化的動詞形式。在查字典的時候看到的，就是動詞原形。例如：

be 是　　　　do 做　　　　work 工作

live 住　　　come 來　　　like 喜歡

2. 第三人稱單數現在式

　　如果進行這個動作的是一個單數的第三人稱主詞（it、she、he等），而且是在「現在」進行這個動作，就用這種動詞變化形式。那麼這種動詞應該是長什麼樣子呢？

1. 一般情況：詞尾 + s

動詞原形	第三人稱單數現在式
work 工作	works
look 看	looks
want 想要	wants

2. 以-ch、-sh、-s、-x、-o 結尾的單字：詞尾 + es

動詞原形	第三人稱單數現在式
teach 教	teaches
wash 洗	washes
dress 打扮	dresses
fix 修理	fixes
go 去	goes

3. 以「子音字母 + y」結尾的單字：把 y 變成 i，再加 es

動詞原形	第三人稱單數現在式
fly 飛翔	flies
cry 哭	cries
try 嘗試	tries

3. 過去式和過去分詞

　　如果講的是過去的事，動詞就要用過去式。那什麼時候用過去分詞呢？它可以用在「完成式」（接在 has 或 have 後面）和「被動式」（接在 be 動詞的後面）。完成式講的是過去一段時間內做完，過了那段時間就不再做的事，而被動式則是用在說一個人、事、物身上「被做了某個動作」的時候。這些在Unit 11會講得更詳細喔！

　　用在完成式和被動式的過去分詞和過去式，大部分的時候都長得一樣，但是也有些特殊狀況會出現不同的變化。這種時候，只能努力把它背起來囉！本書最後面有個「不規則動詞變化表」，可以參考喔！

1. 一般情況：詞尾 + ed

動詞原形	過去式和過去分詞
walk 走	walked
work 工作	worked
help 幫忙	helped

2. 以不發音的字母 e 結尾的單字：詞尾+ d

動詞原形	過去式和過去分詞
decide 決定	decided
hope 希望	hoped
like 喜歡	liked

（也可以想做詞尾的e共用喔！）

3. 以「子音字母 + y」結尾的單字：把 y 變成 i，再加 ed

動詞原形	過去式和過去分詞
carry 搬運	carried
hurry 快	hurried
study 學習	studied

4. 以重音、封閉的音節結尾，而且尾音只有一個子音的單字：把字尾的那個子音寫兩次 + ed

動詞原形	過去式和過去分詞
stop 停	stopped
nod 點頭	nodded
plan 計畫	planned

要注意喔！

以上介紹的都是過去式和過去分詞的規則變化，也就是教你怎麼在動詞原形後面順利加上 -ed。可是，其實還有很多動詞的過去式和過去分詞不是加上 −ed就好了喔！這些是不規則的動詞。例如：

1. 動詞原形、過去式、過去分詞形式都相同：

切割：**cut**（原形）、**cut**（過去式），**cut**（過去分詞）

2. 過去式與過去分詞形式相同，但都不是加 -ed：

帶來：**bring**（原形）、**brought**（過去式）、
　　　brought（過去分詞）

3. 動詞原形、過去式、過去分詞都長得不一樣：

去：**go**（原形）、**went**（過去式）、
　　gone（過去分詞）

這些不規則的變化需要一個一個慢慢記起來。更多不規則動詞的變化都可以在附錄裡找到喔！

（ 4. 現在進行式和現在分詞 ）

在說到現在正在發生、在進行的動作時，就要用be 動詞 + 現在分詞，在時

態上我們稱為「現在進行式」。分詞的形式通常都是在詞尾加上 -ing，但光是加這個 -ing 也有很大的學問喔！快來看看單字不同，加 -ing 的方法有什麼不同？

1. 一般情況：詞尾 + ing

動詞原形	現在分詞
go 去	going
ask 問	asking
play 玩	playing

2. 以不發音的字母 e 結尾的單字：去掉 e，再加 –ing

動詞原形	現在分詞
write 寫	writing
come 來	coming
take 帶走	taking

3. 以重音、封閉的音節結尾，而且末尾字尾只有一個字母的單字：把字尾寫兩次，再加上 –ing

動詞原形	現在分詞
cut 切	cutting
run 跑	running
nod 點頭	nodding

（更多關於時態的介紹，請看Unit 11喔！）

1. 在下面的句子中找出動詞，在下面畫線。

例 All birds _lay_ eggs.
所有的鳥都會下蛋。

1. The flowers smell sweet.

2. Stone is a hard material.

3. Danger! Do not enter.

4. The bus stops.

5. Can you cut the apple into two halves?

2. 寫出下列動詞的第三人稱單數現在式。

例 do _does_

1. catch _____   2. go _____   3. try _____

4. finish _____   5. cross _____   6. mix _____

7. wash _____   8. touch _____   9. hurry _____

3. 寫出下列動詞的過去式和過去分詞。

動詞原形	過去式	過去分詞
do	did	done
drop		
go		
begin		

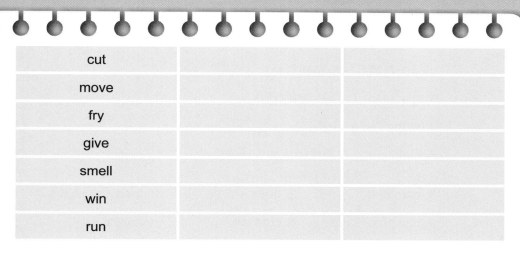

cut		
move		
fry		
give		
smell		
win		
run		

4. 把括號裡面的動詞換成現在分詞，填在空格中。

例 **What are you <u>doing</u> (do)?**
你在做什麼？

1. The ball is _____ (move) towards the hole.

2. The horse is _____ (run) very fast.

3. "What is Susan doing now?"

   "Oh, she is _____ (fly) a kite with her brother."

4. The patient is _____ (die). No one can save him.

你做對了嗎？

1.	1. smell（花聞起來很香。）
	2. is（石頭是一種堅硬的材料。）
	3. Do, enter（危險！請勿進入。）
	4. stops（公車停了。）
	5. Can, cut（你能把蘋果切成兩半嗎？）

2.	1. catches	2. goes	3. tries（去y加ies）
	4. finishes	5. crosses	6. mixes
	7. washes	8. touches	9. hurries（去y加ies）

3.

動詞原形	過去式	過去分詞
do	did	done
drop	dropped	dropped
go	went	gone
begin	began	begun
cut	cut	cut
move	moved	moved
fry	fried	fried
give	gave	given

smell	smelt / smelled	smelt / smelled
win	won	won
run	ran	run

4.	1. moving（球正朝著小洞那邊過去。）
	2. running（這匹馬正在飛奔。）
	3. flying（「蘇珊現在在做什麼？」「她在和弟弟放風箏。」）
	4. dying（病人快死了。沒人能救得了他。）

♥ 確實了解每一題後，再進行下一章喔！

Unit 11.
動詞的時態

Unit 11. 動詞的時態

① 什麼是時態？

英文所說的「時態」，就是用動詞的形式變化來表示不同時間內發生的動作或當時的狀態。英文裡面每一句話都至少會包含一種時態，而且時態對每句話的意思影響都很大，所以認識時態就真的很重要了喔！最常見的時態有六種，下面讓我們一一來認識它們吧！

② 一般現在式

一般現在式通常表示經常發生的動作或存在的常態、事實。例如：

I am a pupil.
我是一個小學生。

You are very kind.
你人真好。

We go to school every day.
我們每天都去上學。

Emma teaches English.
艾瑪教英語。

1. 使用be動詞的一般現在式

1. 第一人稱單數（I）+ am

I am a doctor.
我是一名醫生。

I am hungry.
我餓了。

2. 第三人稱單數（he / she / it）+ is

He is a singer.
他是一位歌手。

She is a kind teacher.
她是一位和藹的老師。

It is cloudy today.
今天是陰天。

3. 第二人稱單數（you）或各人稱的複數（we / you / they）**+ are**

You are a handsome boy.
你是一個帥氣的男孩。

They are busy with their homework every day.
他們每天都忙著寫功課。

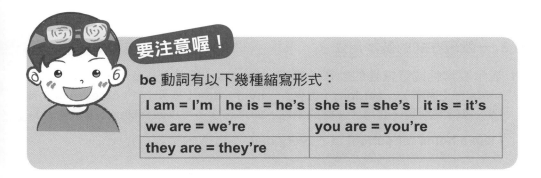

要注意喔！

be 動詞有以下幾種縮寫形式：

I am = I'm	he is = he's	she is = she's	it is = it's
we are = we're		you are = you're	
they are = they're			

2. 使用實義動詞的一般現在式

1. 第三人稱單數（he / she / it）**+** 動詞第三人稱單數現在式

Ann gets up at 8 o'clock every morning.
安每天早上八點起床。

She studies hard.
她很認真讀書。

2. 第一、二人稱單數（I / you）和各人稱的複數（we / you / they）**+** 動詞原形

We want to take a trip during the holiday.
我們想在假期去旅行。

You do a very good job at cooking.
你的廚藝很棒。

They all run fast in the sports meet.
他們在運動會上跑得都很快。

（動詞第三人稱單數現在式，如果忘記了再翻回p.141複習一下吧！）

要注意喔！

be 動詞除了自己可以單獨在句子裡使用外，也可以和其他的動詞一起出現，作為助動詞，不過這種時候句子的時態就會和 be 動詞單獨出現時不一樣了。在後面講解時態的地方，我們會進一步介紹喔！

3. 一般現在式的基本用法

1. 表示經常性或習慣性的動作，常與 always（總是）、often（經常）、usually（通常）、seldom（很少）、every day（每天）、sometimes（有時）等時間副詞一起用。（時間副詞，如果忘記了可以回到Unit 5複習喔！）

I leave home for school at 7 every day.
我每天七點鐘離開家去上學。

Bob always helps the old man.
鮑伯總是會幫助這位老人。

It seldom rains in summer here.
這裡夏天很少下雨。

We usually go home on foot.
我們通常走路回家。

They sometimes go swimming on Sundays.
他們有時候會在禮拜天去游泳。

2. 表示永恆不變的事實或真理。

A bird flies with wings.
鳥用翅膀飛翔。

Taipei lies in the north of Taiwan.
台北位於台灣北部。

3. 用在格言、諺語中。

Pride goes before a fall.
驕者必敗。

Knowledge is power.
知識就是力量。

要注意喔！

在口語中，一般現在式也可以拿來說即將發生的動作或按照計劃來看應該將會發生的動作。例如：

I'm off.
我走啦。

We start school tomorrow.
我們明天開學。

3. 一般過去式

　　一般過去式通常表示過去時間發生的動作或過去曾經存在的狀態。例如：

Mr. Wilson was a professor.
威爾遜先生以前是教授。

There were wolves in the woods.
這片森林裡以前曾經有過狼。

He had a new car.
他以前有輛新車。

They bought beautiful dresses for the party.
她們為聚會買了漂亮的裙子。

1. 使用 be 動詞的一般過去式

1. 第一人稱單數（I）/ 第三人稱單數（he / she / it）+ was

I was sick last night.
昨天晚上我生病了。

She was in Hong Kong some years ago.
她幾年前在香港。

2. 第二人稱單數（you）/ 各人稱複數（we / you / they）+ were

You were the tallest student in our class last semester.
上學期你是班上最高的學生。（the tallest是形容詞最高級的用法）

They were ready to go out, but it started raining.
他們準備好要出門了，但開始下雨了。

2. 使用實義動詞的一般過去式

1. 各人稱單 / 複數都一樣直接加上動詞的過去式

The wicked queen gave Snow White a poisoned apple.
邪惡的皇后給了白雪公主一個有毒的蘋果。

We visited our uncle last week.
我們上禮拜去拜訪了叔叔。

3. 一般過去式的基本用法

1. 表示過去發生的動作或曾經存在的狀態，常與表示過去的時間詞語例如
yesterday（昨天）、last week（上星期）、an hour ago（一小時前）等連用。

The panda gave birth to a baby last Tuesday.
大熊貓上禮拜二生下了一隻小熊貓。

Dad took me to the Carnival yesterday.
昨天爸爸帶我去參加嘉年華會。

2. 表示在過去一段時間裡，經常發生或習慣性的動作或狀態。

I watched the World Cup every day last month.
上個月我每天都看世界盃足球賽。

I collected coins when I was a child.
我小時候有收集硬幣的習慣。

要注意喔！

一般過去式有時候可以用來表示一種客氣、禮貌的語氣。
例如：

I wondered if you could help me.
我想知道您是否能幫我。

4. 一般未來式

一般未來式通常表示現在還沒有發生，但以後會發生的事情或動作。例如：

I shall be ten years old next year.
我明年就十歲了。

John will go to America next week.
約翰下星期會去美國。

Will you go to the party tonight?
你今天晚上會去參加派對嗎？

We will take this cap.
我們要買這頂帽子。

1. 一般未來式的形式

1. 第一人稱（I / we）+ shall + 動詞原形

I shall be there in five minutes.
我五分鐘後就會到那裡了。

Where shall we go tonight?
我們今天晚上要去哪裡？

We shall probably go to Hawaii for our holiday.
我們很有可能去夏威夷度假。

2. 各人稱單複數 + will + 動詞原形

When will we know our test scores?
我們什麼時候才會知道我們考試的分數？

Philip will go fishing with his father tomorrow.
明天菲利普要和他爸爸去釣魚。

You will get sick if you eat too much.
如果吃太多，你會生病喔。

It will rain this afternoon.
今天下午會下雨。

要注意喔！

1. 用未來式時，只有第一人稱（I / we）後面可以接 shall，因為 shall 有表達自己「打算要怎麼做」的意思，而你不清楚其他人是怎麼打算的，所以就不能接著第二、第三人稱用 shall 這個字了。

此外，I / we shall 與 I / we will 都表示「我（們）將……」的意思，可以通用。例如：

We shall have a game of chess after tea.

= We will have a game of chess after tea.

喝完茶我們要去下棋。

2. will、shall 都可以縮寫成「'll」。例如：

I shall / I will = I'll   you will = you'll

she will = she'll   it will = it'll

2. 一般未來式的基本用法

　　一般未來式表示將要發生的事情或動作，所以經常與表示未來時間的詞語 連用，像是 tomorrow（明天）、next time / week / month / year（下次 / 下星期 / 下個月 / 明年）、in a few minutes / hours / days / weeks（幾分鐘後 / 幾小時後 / 幾天後 / 幾星期後）。

He'll be back tomorrow.
他明天會回來。

They will complete the classroom building next month.
他們下個月就會把這棟教學大樓蓋好了。

I will leave in five minutes.
我五分鐘後就走。

Will you come back to see us next year?
明年你會回來看我們嗎？

　　此外，一般未來式還有一個「be going to +動詞」形式的用法。這個形式大多用於表示打算、計畫和安排好的事情，也可以表示即將要發生的動作或情況。例如：

Karl is going to have a bath.
卡爾要去洗澡了。

They are going to clean the house.
他們打算打掃房子。

Are you going to watch the program tonight?
你今晚要看那個節目嗎？

要注意喔！

徵求其他人意見時，一般可以用「Shall I / we...」的句型。例如：

Shall I open the window?
我可以打開窗戶嗎？

Shall we go?
我們可以走了嗎？

5. 現在進行式

現在進行式主要用來表示正在進行或發生的動作。例如：

I am eating at the table.
我正在桌子旁邊吃飯。

She is cooking in the kitchen.
她正在廚房煮飯。

It is snowing now.
現在正在下雪。

They are having a picnic in the park.
他們正在公園裡野餐。

1. 現在進行式的形式

1. 第一人稱單數（I）+ am + 現在分詞

I am reading a book.
我正在看書。

I am learning how to swim.
我正在學游泳。

2. 第三人稱單數（he / she / it）+ is + 現在分詞

He is cleaning the room.
他正在打掃房間。

Miss White is listening to music.
懷特小姐正在聽音樂。

3. 第二人稱單數（you）或各人稱複數（we / you / they）+ are + 現在分詞

Are you doing your homework, Amy?
艾咪，妳在寫功課嗎？

The girls are singing.
女孩們正在唱歌。

We are sitting around the Christmas tree.
我們正圍坐在聖誕樹旁。

（現在分詞，我們在p.144介紹過，不熟的話先複習一下吧！）

2. 現在進行式的基本用法

1. 表示「現在」（說這句話的人正在說話時）正在發生的事情，常與 now（現在）、at present（目前）、today（今天）等時間狀語連用。

My father is playing chess with my uncle now.
我爸爸現在正在和我叔叔下棋。

Be quiet, please. Mom is sleeping.
請安靜點。媽媽正在睡覺。

We are singing and dancing now.
我們現在又唱又跳。

2. 表示最近這段時間內正在進行的動作（說話時不一定有在做），常與 this week（這星期）、this month（這個月）、these days（這一陣子）等表達「最近這段時間」的詞語連用。

The scientist is doing an experiment this week.
這位科學家這星期在做一個實驗。

We are writing a book this month.
我們這個月有在寫一本書。

要注意喔！

1. 現在進行式也可以用來表示按照計劃將要發生的動作。要表達這種情形時，常用的動詞有 **come**、**go**、**leave**、**start** 等。例如：

   George is coming soon.
   喬治快到了。

   I'm leaving by train tonight.
   我今天晚上會坐火車離開。

2. 現在式也可以表示「發生變化的過程」。例如：

   The trees are growing taller.
   這些樹越長越高了。

   It is getting dark. Let's go home.
   天漸漸黑了，我們回家吧。

6. 現在完成式

現在完成式通常表示過去的某一段時間內發生過的動作或狀態。這個動作過了那段時間之後就沒有再做了，不過對於之後的狀況可能會有一點影響。例如：

I have already had lunch.
我已經吃過午飯了。

（表示之前有吃，現在沒有在吃，而且現在不餓，不用再吃了）

Mary has been to Europe before.
瑪麗以前去過歐洲。

（表示去過歐洲，但現在已經不在那裡了。不過因為去過，所以她瞭解歐洲的情況）

They have not arrived yet.
他們還沒到。

（表示他們還沒有完成「到達」這個動作，也就是現在不在這裡）

Tim has been ill.
提姆生病了。

（表示提姆有一段時間都在生病）

1. 現在完成式的形式

1. 第一、二人稱單數（I / you）與各人稱複數（we / you / they）+ have + 過去分詞

They have been in Beijing since 2004.
他們從 2004 年起就一直在北京。

I have been to many countries.
我去過許多國家。

2. 第三人稱單數（he / she / it）+ has + 過去分詞

Tom has been absent for three days.
湯姆已經三天沒來了。

She has gone to the town.
她進城去了。

2. 現在完成式的基本用法

1. 表示過去發生的動作（動作已結束）對現在的影響，常與 already（已經）、just（剛剛）、yet（還）、ever（曾經）、never（從來沒有）等表示時間的副詞連用。

Mary has already invited us to her birthday party on Sunday.
瑪麗已經邀請我們這禮拜天去參加她的生日聚會。

（對現在的影響：既然瑪麗已經邀了我們，我們禮拜天就不能做其他事情了）

He has locked the door.
他已經把門鎖上了。

（對現在的影響：既然他已經把門鎖起來了，門就打不開了）

2. 表示從過去一直持續到現在的動作或狀態，常與 since（自從某個時間開始）、for（總共過了多少時間）等詞一起出現。

He has been an engineer for 3 years.
他已經做了三年的工程師了。

（這三年一直持續到現在都在做工程師）

They have been in the classroom since 2 o'clock.
他們兩點以後就一直在教室裡。

(從兩點開始就一直持續到現在都在教室)

要注意喔!

常常有人搞不清楚「have been to」與「have gone to」的區別,因為它們都是「已經去過」的意思不是嗎?那它們到底應該怎麼分呢?很簡單!「have been to」表示「去過某個地方,已經回來了」;「have gone to」表示「去了某個地方,還沒有回來」。例如:

He has been to America.
他去美國了。(現在已經去完美國回來了,人在這裡)
He has gone to America.
他去美國了。(已經去美國了,人還在美國,不在這裡)

7. 過去進行式

過去進行時通常是表示在過去某一段時間內正在進行或發生的動作。例如:

I was watching TV at 4:00 p.m. yesterday.
昨天下午 4 點我在看電視。

Emily was having classes yesterday morning.
艾蜜莉昨天早上都在上課。

They were building a bridge last year.
他們去年在蓋一座橋。

We were doing our homework at 8:00 last night.
昨天晚上八點我們正在寫功課。

1. 過去進行時的形式

1. 第一人稱單數(I)或第三人稱單數(he / she / it)+ was + 現在分詞

Ten minutes ago, I was sitting in the classroom.
十分鐘前,我正坐在教室。

It was raining last week.
上星期一直有在下雨。

2. 第二人稱單數（you）和各人稱複數（we / you / they）+ were + 現在分詞

Lucy and Ann were peeling apples.
露西和安之前在削蘋果。

What were you doing at nine last night?
昨晚九點的時候你在幹嘛？

1. 過去進行式的基本用法

1. 表示過去某個時刻正在進行著的動作，常與 at 7 o'clock（在七點）、at that time（在那個時候）等表示具體時間的詞語一起用。

Dad was washing the car at 7:30 yesterday morning.
昨天早上 7 點半的時候，爸爸正在洗車。

They were picking apples in the garden at that time.
那個時候他們正在果園裡採蘋果。

2. 表示過去某一段時間內一直在進行的動作，常與 last week（上星期）、last year（去年）等表示過去的一段時間的詞語一起用。

We were painting a picture last week.
上個星期我們在畫一幅畫。

I was living in my hometown last year.
去年我待在家鄉。

要注意喔！

過去進行式還可以與由「when」開始的時間子句一起用，表示「在那個時候，正在……」的意思。例如：

Patrick was cooking when the telephone rang.
當電話鈴響的時候，派崔克正在做飯。

Most people were sleeping when the earthquake happened.
地震發生的時候，大部分的人都在睡覺。

1. 用 am, is 或 are 填空看看吧！

例 **Penguins _are_ animals.**
企鵝是一種動物。

1. I _____ Peter. I _____ ten years old.

2. Martin _____ a football player.

3. Excuse me. _____ you Mr. Baker?

4. Tom and Dick _____ good friends. They _____ in the same class.

5. The dolphin（海豚）_____ a sea animal.

2. 把括弧內的動詞改成一般現在式，填到空格裡。

例 **We _have_ (have) breakfast at 7:00 a.m.**
我們早晨七點吃早飯。

1. Mom _____ (work) in a company.

2. Polar bears _____ (live) in the North Pole.

3. Miss White _____ (teach) us English.

4. Farmers _____ (have) a good harvest this year.

5. Mr. Lee doesn't _____ (like) butter and cheese.

6. My shoes _____ (be) dirty. They _____ (need) polishing.

3. 把括弧內最正確的字圈起來。

例 **A Mr. Smith (call, calls, (called)) you yesterday.**
昨天有位史密斯先生打電話給你。

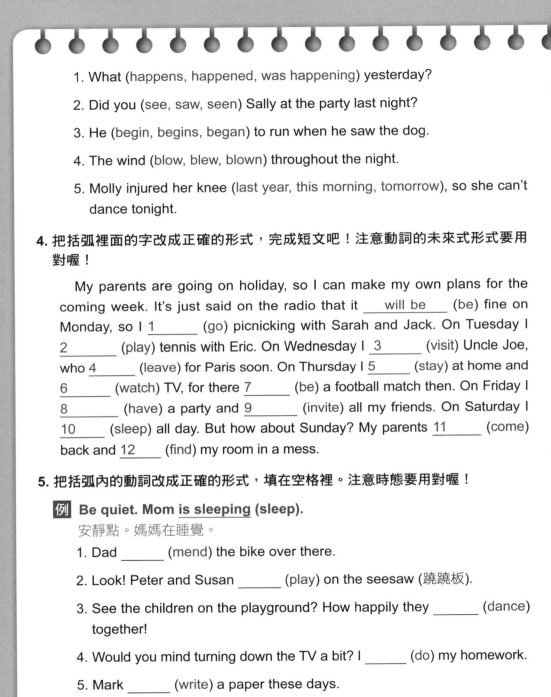

1. What (happens, happened, was happening) yesterday?

2. Did you (see, saw, seen) Sally at the party last night?

3. He (begin, begins, began) to run when he saw the dog.

4. The wind (blow, blew, blown) throughout the night.

5. Molly injured her knee (last year, this morning, tomorrow), so she can't dance tonight.

4. 把括弧裡面的字改成正確的形式，完成短文吧！注意動詞的未來式形式要用對喔！

My parents are going on holiday, so I can make my own plans for the coming week. It's just said on the radio that it ___will be___ (be) fine on Monday, so I 1_____ (go) picnicking with Sarah and Jack. On Tuesday I 2_____ (play) tennis with Eric. On Wednesday I 3_____ (visit) Uncle Joe, who 4_____ (leave) for Paris soon. On Thursday I 5____ (stay) at home and 6_____ (watch) TV, for there 7_____ (be) a football match then. On Friday I 8_____ (have) a party and 9_____ (invite) all my friends. On Saturday I 10____ (sleep) all day. But how about Sunday? My parents 11_____ (come) back and 12____ (find) my room in a mess.

5. 把括弧內的動詞改成正確的形式，填在空格裡。注意時態要用對喔！

例 **Be quiet. Mom is sleeping (sleep).**
安靜點。媽媽在睡覺。

1. Dad _____ (mend) the bike over there.

2. Look! Peter and Susan _____ (play) on the seesaw (蹺蹺板).

3. See the children on the playground? How happily they _____ (dance) together!

4. Would you mind turning down the TV a bit? I _____ (do) my homework.

5. Mark _____ (write) a paper these days.

6. 把括弧內錯誤或不適合的答案劃掉。

例 (Have, ~~Did~~) you (~~watered~~, water) the flowers yet?
你澆花了嗎?

1. The Browns (lived, have lived) in Taichung since 1997.

2. (Have, Do) you (seen, see) Julia recently?

3. (Have, Did) you (finish, finished) your homework?

4. Wait a minute. They (haven't arrived, don't arrive) yet.

5. John, I (didn't see, haven't seen) you for two weeks!

7. 從下面的 a～f 選擇意思最符合的一項,把序號填在每一句的橫線上,把句子補完吧!每個選項只能用一次。

例 I was talking on the phone ___a___.
你按門鈴的時候我在接電話。

1. What were you doing _____?

2. Dad was reading a newspaper at seven o'clock _____.

3. They were building a railway _____.

4. All the guests were drinking champagne(香檳)and _____.

5. Were you cleaning the room while _____?

a. when you rang the doorbell

b. at that moment

c. eating sandwiches

d. last year

e. Jane was doing the dishes

f. yesterday evening

參考解答

你做對了嗎？

1.

1. am；am（我是彼得，我十歲了。）

2. is（馬丁是一名足球運動員。）

3. Are（打擾一下，請問您是貝克先生嗎？）

4. are；are（湯姆和迪克是好朋友。他們同班。）

5. is（海豚是一種海洋動物。）

2.

1. works（媽媽在一家公司上班。）

2. live（北極熊住在北極。）

3. teaches（懷特小姐教我們英文。）

4. have（農民們今年收穫很不錯。）

5. like（李先生不喜歡奶油和乳酪。）
（注意：否定doesn't後面要用動詞原形like）

6. are；need（我的鞋子髒了，該擦了。）

3.

1. happened（昨天發生了什麼事？）

2. see（昨晚你在派對有看到莎莉嗎？）
（注意：疑問句中，助動詞did後面要用動詞原形see）

3. began（他一看到那隻狗就開始逃跑。）

4. blew（風吹了一整晚。）

5. this morning
（莫莉今天早上弄傷了膝蓋，所以今晚不能跳舞了。）

4.

My parents are going on holiday, so I can make my own plans for the coming week. It's just said on the radio that it __will be__ fine on Monday, so I _1_ __am going__ picnicking with Sarah and Jack. On Tuesday I _2_ __am going to play__ tennis with Eric. On Wednesday I _3_ __am going to visit__ Uncle Joe, who _4_ __is leaving__ for Paris soon. On Thursday I _5_ __will stay__ at home and _6_ __watch__ TV, for there _7_ __will be__ a football match then. On Friday I _8_ __am going to have__ a party and _9_ __am going to invite__ all my friends. On Saturday I _10_ __will sleep__ all day. But what about Sunday? My parents _11_ __will come__ back and _12_ __find__ my room in a mess.

5.

1. is mending（爸爸正在那裡修腳踏車。）

2. are playing（你看！彼得和蘇珊正在玩蹺蹺板。）

3. are dancing
   （看到操場上的那些小孩了嗎？他們跳舞跳得多開心啊！）

4. am doing（你可以把電視的聲音調低一點嗎？我在寫作業耶。）

5. is writing（馬克這一陣子都在寫論文。）

6.

1. (lived, have lived)（布朗一家自從1997年就住在台中。）

2. (Have, Do)；(seen, see)（你最近有看到茱麗亞嗎？）

3. (Have, Did)；(finish, finished)（你功課寫完了嗎？）

4. (haven't arrived, don't arrive)（等一下，他們還沒到。）

5. (didn't see, haven't seen)（約翰，我有兩個禮拜沒見到你了！）

7.

1. b（那個時候你們在做什麼？）

2. f（爸爸昨天晚上七點在看報紙。）

3. d（他們去年在蓋一條鐵路。）

4. c（所有的客人都在喝香檳、吃三明治。）

5. e（珍妮在洗碗的時候，你在打掃房間嗎？）

♥ 確實了解每一題後，再進行下一章喔！

Unit 12.
直述句

Unit 12. 直述句

1. 什麼是直述句？

直述句就是簡單直接地陳述一件事情或表達一種看法的句子。它的結尾用句號，在講這種句子的時候音調一般不會有什麼太大的起起伏伏。

The telephone rang.
電話響了。（説明一個事實）

I really agree.
我真的同意。（表達一種看法）

We won't go to school tomorrow.
我們明天不去上學。（陳述一個事實）

I don't think so.
我不這麼覺得。（表達一種看法）

2. 直述句的分類

1. 肯定形式的直述句

直述句的肯定形式有以下兩種結構：

1. 主詞 + 謂語 + 其他

Susan likes skating in winter.
蘇珊喜歡在冬天溜冰。

Martin is reading.
馬丁正在讀書。

Tom played basketball yesterday.
湯姆昨天有打籃球。

You must look after your things.
你必須自己管好自己的東西。

2. 主詞 + be 動詞 + 主詞補語

The fridge is empty.
冰箱是空的。

> **主詞**：每一個句子，都有被陳述、被説明的對象，這個對象就稱為「主詞」。
>
> **謂語**：相對於被説明的「對象」，對此對象的加以陳述、説明，就稱之為「謂語」。
>
> **主詞補語**：用來補足主詞意義的詞，如：表示主詞的狀態、特徵、身分，或其他補充説明，都是「主詞補語」。

This is our classroom.
這是我們的教室。

Milk and eggs are good for your health.
牛奶和雞蛋對你的健康有好處。

We are good friends.
我們是好朋友。

要注意喔！

「**There be 句型**」也是一種很重要的直述句型，主要表示「在什麼地方存在什麼事物」。例如：
There is a table in the room.
房間裏有一張桌子。

有關「**there be 句型**」，我們會在Unit 16更詳細介紹喔！

2. 否定形式的直述句

否定形式的句子中含有否定詞（否定詞就是表示有否定意思的詞，最常見的否定詞是 no 和 not）。常見的否定形式有以下四種：

1. 如果句子裡的動詞是 be 動詞，就用「be + not」構成否定形式。

Diana is not a student.
黛安娜不是學生。

I'm not busy now.
我現在不忙。

It was not cloudy yesterday.
昨天不是陰天。

They were not at home last night.
他們昨天晚上不在家。

2 如果句子裡的動詞是實義動詞，而且句子裡也沒有情態動詞或助動詞，就用「do / does / did + not」構成否定形式。

I do not like music.
我不喜歡音樂。

He does not have a partner for the tennis class.
他網球課沒有搭檔。

The farmer did not want to shoot the rabbit.
這個農夫並沒有想開槍射兔子。

3. 如果句子裡有「助動詞 + 實義動詞」，就用「助動詞 + not」構成否定。

I am not going to play computer games.
我不打算玩電腦遊戲。

I have not finished my homework.
我功課還沒有寫完。

Mary has not been to the Great Wall.
瑪麗沒有去過長城。

4. 如果句子裡有「情態動詞 + 實義動詞」，就用「情態動詞 + not」構成否定。

You must not go there.
你不可以去那裡。

You should not stay up too late.
你不應該熬夜。

We cannot go swimming with you this weekend.
這週末我們不能跟你去游泳。

要注意喔！

請記住這些否定形式的縮寫，這些都常常會用到喔！

is not = isn't are not = aren't	will not = won't shall not = shan't
was not = wasn't were not = weren't	should not = shouldn't
do not = don't does not = doesn't	cannot = can't must not = mustn't
have not = haven't has not = hasn't	need not = needn't did not = didn't

1. 根據中文意思，把每題給的單字按正確順序排好，組成一個肯定句。

例 to, Philip, morning, every, goes, work

Philip goes to work every morning.

菲利普每天早上都去上班。

1. 妮娜喉嚨痛。

sore, a, Nina, throat, has

_____.

2. 滑雪是我最喜愛的運動。

skiing, my, sport, is, favorite

_____.

3. 我們明天早上七點在學校門口見。

seven o'clock, shall, morning, at, we, tomorrow, gate, meet, the, school, at

_____.

4. 跑車比摩托車快。

faster, a, than, car, is, sports, a, motorbike

_____.

5. 亨利太小，還不能自己照顧自己。

look after, too, Henry, himself, to, young, is

_____.

6. 就在這時，青蛙變成了一位年輕英俊的王子。

young, changed, the, Prince, frog, at that moment, a, handsome, into

_____.

2. 根據括弧內的提示，把肯定句變為否定句。

例 **This isn't (be) my book.**
這不是我的書。

1. The cartoon _____ (be) very interesting.

2. Nina _____ (do) like jelly.

3. Kobe _____ (be) a good football player, but he is a good basketball player.

4. The ostrich _____ (can) fly, but it can run very fast.

5. Children _____ (should) play on the road.

6. You _____ (must) smoke in this area.

7. He _____ (do) go to school because he had a cold.

8. Sue is ill. She _____ (will) be at the party tonight.

1.	1. Nina has a sore throat.
	2. Skiing is my favorite sport.
	3. We shall meet at the school gate at seven o'clock tomorrow morning.
	4. A sports car is faster than a motorbike.
	5. Henry is too young to look after himself.
	6. At that moment the frog changed into a handsome young Prince.
2.	1. isn't（這個動畫片不是很有趣。）
	2. doesn't（妮娜不喜歡果凍。）
	3. isn't（柯比足球踢得不好，但是籃球打得很好。）
	4. can't（鴕鳥不會飛，但是牠跑得非常快。）
	5. shouldn't（孩子們不應該在馬路上玩耍。）
	6. mustn't（你不能在這一區吸煙。）
	7. didn't（他沒有去上學，因為他感冒了。）
	8. won't（蘇生病了。她今晚不會參加派對了。）

♥ 確實了解每一題後，再進行下一章喔！

Unit 13.
疑問句

Unit 13. 疑問句

① 什麼是疑問句？

用來提出問題的句子叫做疑問句。要認出疑問句其實很簡單，只要句子最後面是問號的，就是疑問句囉。例如：

Are you a teacher?
你是老師嗎？

What are you looking for?
你在找什麼？

Are your new clothes red or black?
你的新衣服是紅色的還是黑色的？

It's a fine day, isn't it?
天氣真好，不是嗎？

② 疑問句的種類

疑問句有四種：一般疑問句、特殊疑問句、選擇疑問句、反意疑問句。這些有什麼差別呢？

1. 一般疑問句

一般疑問句通常是以 be、have、助動詞或情態動詞開頭，回答時用 Yes 或 No。在講這些句子的時候，句子最後的音調是上揚的。例如：

Are you from Germany?
你來自德國嗎？

May I borrow your ruler?
我能借用你的尺嗎？

Have you (got) a bike?
你有腳踏車嗎？

Does he often swim in summer?
他夏天常常去游泳嗎？

Will you go to the park tomorrow?
你明天會去公園嗎？

→ 一般疑問句的回答方式

一般疑問句通常都是問「是不是？」、「有沒有」？所以如果答案是肯定的，就回答 Yes，後面接肯定的句子；而如果答案是否定的，就回答 No，後面接否定的句子。例如：

—**Do you like dogs?**
你喜歡狗嗎？

—**Yes, I do.**
是的，我喜歡。

—**No, I don't.**
不，我不喜歡

要注意喔！

一般疑問句都有一定的形式喔！把這三種常見的句子形式背起來吧！

1. **Am / Is / Are / Was / Were** + 主詞 + 其他 + ?
2. **Do / Does / Did / Will / Shall / Can / May / Must** + 主詞 + 動詞原形 + 其他 + ?
3. **Have / Has / Had** + 主詞 + 動詞過去分詞 + 其他 + ?

2. 特殊疑問句

特殊疑問句是對句子中某一部分提問的疑問句，可能是問地點、時間、對象……等等。常以疑問詞 who、who、whose、what、which、when、why、where、how 等開頭。講這些句子時，一般開頭的地方音調比較高。例如：

Carl is our friend.
卡爾是我們的朋友。

Who is our friend?
誰是我們的朋友？

這裡就是把主詞「Carl」換成「who」（誰）來提出問題。

Ken plays basketball on Sundays.
肯在星期天打籃球。

What does Ken do on Sundays?
肯星期天都做什麼？

　　這裡就是把 play basketball 這件肯星期天很喜歡做的事換掉，換成「do what」（做什麼）。看起來很複雜嗎？沒關係，下面會說得更詳細喔！

1. 用 What 開頭的特殊疑問句，常用來詢問「什麼」。

What's the time now, Jack?
傑克，現在幾點了？

What color is the car?
這輛汽車是什麼顏色？

What's the weather like today?
今天天氣怎麼樣？

What did you do last night?
你昨天晚上做什麼？

2. 用 Who 開頭的特殊疑問句，通常用來詢問「誰」。

Who's that old man?
那位老人是誰？

Who is coming today?
今天誰會來？

Who can help me?
誰能幫我？

Who told you the news?
誰告訴你這個消息的？

3. 用 Whose 開頭的特殊疑問句，通常用來詢問「誰的」。

Whose wallet is this?
這是誰的錢包？

Whose cat is it?
這是誰的貓？

Whose coats are these?
這些是誰的外套？

Whose glasses are those?
那些是誰的眼鏡？

4. 用 Which 開頭的特殊疑問句，通常用來詢問「哪一個」。

Which color do you like?
你喜歡哪一種顏色？

Which grade is Sue in?
蘇念哪個年級（幾年級）？

Which book are you reading?
你在看哪本書？

Which bag will they buy?
他們要買哪個包包？

5. 用 **When** 開頭的特殊疑問句，通常用來詢問「什麼時候」。

When shall we have a barbecue?
我們什麼時候烤肉？

When are you taking me to the zoo, Mom?
媽媽，妳什麼時候要帶我去動物園？

When did he go out?
他什麼時候出去的？

When does school begin?
學校什麼時候開學？

6. 用 **Why** 開頭的特殊疑問句，通常用來詢問「為什麼」。

Why are you late?
你為什麼遲到？

Why didn't you finish your homework yesterday?
為什麼你昨天功課沒寫完？

Why is she crying?
她為什麼在哭？

Why don't we go together?
我們為什麼不一起去呢？

7. 用 **Where** 開頭的特殊疑問句，通常用來詢問「在哪裡」。

Where were you last night?
你昨天晚上在哪裡？

Where does Mr. White live?
懷特先生住在哪？

Where shall we meet tomorrow morning?
明天早上我們在哪裡見？

Where did they have a picnic?
他們在哪裡野餐的？

8. 用 How 開頭的特殊疑問句，通常用來詢問「怎麼樣」。

How are you today?
你今天怎麼樣？

（詢問「健康狀況怎樣」）

How do you go to school every day?
你每天怎麼去學校的？

（詢問「怎樣做一件事」）

　　How 還可以和 many、much、long、often等詞一起用，問的事情也就會跟著不一樣。例如：

How many carrots does the rabbit eat?
兔子吃多少根胡蘿蔔？

（詢問數量）

How much is the fish?
魚多少錢？

（詢問價錢）

How long will you stay there?
你要在那裡待多久？

（詢問時間的長短）

How often do they go to the cinema?
他們多常去看電影？

（詢問頻率，「多久一次」）

⮕ **特殊疑問句的回答方式**

　　需注意，特殊疑問句不是問「是不是」、「有沒有」，所以不能只用 Yes 或 No 回答，要根據實際情況直接回答才行。例如：

—**How old are you?**
你幾歲了？

—**I'm forty.**
我四十歲了。

要注意喔！

「whom」也可以當作特殊疑問句的開頭。和「who」一樣也是詢問「誰」，但它只能對句子的受詞提問，對主詞就不行。例如：

Whom are you talking about?
你們正在談論誰？

（talking about + 人，所以被討論的對象要用受詞，因此疑問句用whom問）

3. 選擇疑問句

選擇疑問句就是提供兩種或兩種以上的情況，讓對方選擇。句子裡面通常會有 or，用來連接兩個以上的選項。在說這種句子時，or 前的部分音調上揚，or 後的部分音調較低。例如：

Are you in Class One or in Class Two?
你在一班還是二班？

Is this book yours or hers?
這本書是你的還是她的？

Who do you like best, John, Sam or Dick?
你最喜歡誰，約翰、山姆還是迪克？

Which shirt would you like, the white one or the yellow one?
你想要哪件襯衫，這件白色的還是那件黃色的？

➡ 選擇疑問句的結構

1. 一般疑問句 + or + 選項

Are these apples red or green?
這些蘋果是紅色的還是綠色的？

Do you like tea or coffee?
你喜歡喝茶還是喝咖啡？

Is Dublin the capital of Scotland or Ireland?
都柏林是蘇格蘭的首都還是愛爾蘭的首都？

Did they go to the gym by bike or by bus?
他們是騎腳踏車去健身房，還是坐公車去？

2. 特殊疑問句 + 選項 + or + 選項

Which girl is more beautiful, Sally or Jessica?
莎莉和潔西卡哪個比較漂亮？

Who is Uncle Li, the old one or the young one?
哪位是李伯伯？年輕的那位還是老的那位？

How did you get here, by bike or on foot?
你怎麼來這裡的？是騎車還是用走的？

選擇疑問句的回答方式

選擇疑問句的回答方式跟特殊疑問句類似，不用 Yes 或 No 回答，而是要根據實際情況直接回答你選哪一個。例如：

—**Are your shoes red or blue?**
你的鞋子是紅色的還是藍色的？

—**They're red.**
紅色的。

要注意喔！

一般疑問句後面加「**or not**」的話，就可以構成選擇疑問句（選擇「有沒有」、「要不要」）。例如：
Do you like the new dress or not?
這條新裙子，你喜歡還是不喜歡？
Have you had breakfast or not?
你吃早餐了沒？

4. 反意疑問句

反意疑問句是接在陳述句的後面，對陳述句所說的事實或看法提出疑問的句子。在講這種句子時，陳述句的部分音調較低，附加疑問句語調既可以上升也可以往下。例如：

You know him, don't you?
你認識他，不是嗎？

　　（「You know him,」是陳述句，「don't you」是附加的疑問句）

She has been to London, hasn't she?
她去過倫敦，不是嗎？

Horses can't fly, can they?
馬不會飛，是嗎？

John doesn't like tea, does he?
約翰不喜歡喝茶，是嗎？

反意疑問句的結構

1. 肯定的陳述句 + 否定的附加疑問句

We were late, weren't we?
我們遲到了，不是嗎？

He visited the Science Museum with Ben yesterday, didn't he?
他昨天和阿班參觀了科學博物館，不是嗎？

2 否定的陳述句 + 肯定的附加疑問句

Andy can't speak French, can he?
安迪不會講法文，是嗎？

Susan isn't very busy, is she?
蘇珊沒有很忙，是嗎？

附加疑問句的結構

1. 附加疑問句的主詞必須和陳述句的主詞指的是同一個東西。如果陳述句的主詞是名詞時，附加疑問句的主詞必須使用對應的人稱代名詞。

Amy and Tim are classmates, aren't they?
愛咪和提姆是同學，不是嗎？

　　（愛咪和提姆有兩個人，他們的代名詞就會是「they 他們」）

2. 附加疑問句的時態也必須和陳述句的時態完全一樣。

They went to the cinema, didn't they?
他們去電影院了，不是嗎？

3. 附加的疑問句如果是否定的，都必須用縮寫形式。

It's raining, isn't it?
下雨了，不是嗎？

（不能寫做is not it?←錯誤）

要注意喔！

附加疑問句其實就是一種簡略的一般疑問句。否定附加疑問句的結構，其實和否定句的結構差不多，回頭看看 **Unit 12** 講到否定句的地方，就可以發現了喔！

反意疑問句的回答方式

　　反意疑問句用Yes或No來回答。如果陳述句部分的內容是事實，就用 Yes回答，後面也就用肯定結構；如果陳述句部分的內容不是事實，就用 No 回答，後面跟著用否定結構。例如：

—**You can speak Russian, can't you?**
　你會說俄語，不是嗎？

—**Yes, I can.**
　是，我會。

—**No, I can't.**
　不是，我不會。

—**It isn't hot, is it?**
　沒有很熱嘛，對嗎？

—**Yes, it is.**
　很熱啦。

—**No, it isn't.**
　沒有很熱啊。

練習做做看

1. 下面這些句子是屬於哪種問句呢？請填入正確的答案。

一般疑問句	特殊疑問句	選擇疑問句	反意疑問句

1. Would you like some potatoes? _____

2. Are you coming or not? _____

3. Sally didn't go to the party, did she? _____

4. May I use your computer? _____

5. The cheese has gone bad, hasn't it? _____

6. Who'll be there tomorrow? _____

7. Can you buy me some crayons? _____

8. Susan can speak English quite well, can't she? _____

9. Where should I put these boxes? _____

10. Is the answer right or wrong? _____

11. What do you think of the film? _____

12. How did they get there, by bus or by train? _____

2. 針對下列問題，作簡單的回答。

例 **Is Miss Lee your English teacher?**

Yes, <u>she is.</u> / No, <u>she isn't.</u>

李小姐是你們的英文老師嗎？
是的，她是。/ 不，她不是。

1. Did John pass the exam? Yes, _____.

2. Is there anyone at home? No, _____.

3. Are you enjoying your English lessons? Yes, _____.

4. Is the computer working now? No, _____.

5. Has Mr. Lee come back from his holiday? No, _____.

3. 根據回答，在空格填上適當的疑問詞。

例 **When do the shops open in the morning?**
Nine o'clock.

商店早上幾點開門？九點。

1. _____ is your father? He is a doctor.

2. _____ shall we take a holiday? Next week.

3. _____ are the Greens coming? On Monday.

4. _____ dictionary is this? It's Lily's.

5. _____ is the broom? It's behind the door.

6. _____ is the man with a beard? He is Mr. Black.

7. _____ do you like better, baseball or tennis? Baseball, I think.

8. _____ are you always late? Because of the traffic jam.

4. 將下面的反意疑問句補充完整。

例 **You have read this book, haven't you?**

你看過這本書了，不是嗎？

1. It is a quiet place, _____ it?

2. Lucy didn't go to the party last night, _____ she?

3. Fred doesn't work in a factory, _____ he?

4. The children clean their room themselves, _____ they?

5. You haven't heard from him, _____ you?

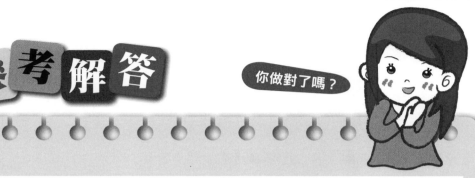

你做對了嗎？

1.	1. Would you like some potatoes?	一般疑問句
	2. Are you coming or not?	選擇疑問句
	3. Sally didn't go to the party, did she?	反意疑問句
	4. May I use your computer?	一般疑問句
	5. The cheese has gone bad, hasn't it?	反意疑問句
	6. Who'll be there tomorrow?	特殊疑問句
	7. Can you buy me some crayons?	一般疑問句
	8. Susan can speak English quite well, can't she?	反意疑問句
	9. Where should I put these boxes?	特殊疑問句
	10. Is the answer right or wrong?	選擇疑問句
	11. What do you think of the film?	特殊疑問句
	12. How did they get there, by bus or by train?	選擇疑問句

2.	1. he did （約翰通過考試了嗎？是的，他通過了。）
	2. there isn't（家裡有人嗎？不，沒有。）
	3. I am / we are（你們喜歡上英文課嗎？是的，我們喜歡。）
	4. it isn't（電腦現在能用了嗎？不，不能。）
	5. he hasn't（李先生已經度假回來了嗎？不，還沒有。）

3.	1. What（你爸爸是做什麼的？他是醫生。）
	2. When（我們什麼時候去度假？下禮拜。）
	3. When（格林一家什麼時候來？星期一。）
	4. Whose（這是誰的字典？是莉莉的。）
	5. Where（掃把在哪裡？在門後面。）
	6. Who（留鬍子的那個人是誰？是布萊克先生。）
	7. Which（棒球和網球，你比較喜歡哪一個？我想是棒球吧。）
	8. Why（你為什麼每次都遲到？因為塞車。）

4.	1. isn't（這裡很安靜，不是嗎？）
	2. did（露西昨晚沒去參加派對，不是嗎？）
	3. does（弗雷德不在工廠工作，是嗎？）
	4. don't（孩子們自己打掃房間，不是嗎？）
	5. have（你還沒跟他聯絡上，是嗎？）

♥ 確實了解每一題後，再進行下一章喔！

Unit 14.
祈使句

Unit 14. 祈使句

1. 什麼是祈使句？

用來表示請求、命令、勸告、建議等的句子就叫做祈使句。祈使句通常沒有主詞，句子最後使用句號或驚嘆號。例如：

Be careful!
小心！

Sit down, please.
請坐。

Turn left and then go straight.
向左轉，然後一直走。

Please turn off the light when you leave.
離開的時候請關燈。

要注意喔！

為什麼祈使句裡面會沒有主詞呢？那是因為既然要命令人、請求人，合理來說，場景應該是面對著對方說話。既然這樣，主詞就乾脆省略掉了。

2. 祈使句的分類

根據用途和功能，祈使句可以分為下面幾類：

1. 表示請求

Close the windows, please.
請把窗戶關上。

Please put it on the table.
請把它放在桌上。

2. 表示命令

Stop talking!
不要講話！

Clean the classroom immediately!
馬上把教室打掃乾淨！

3. 表示提醒或警告

Be careful! The soup is hot.
小心！湯很燙。

Look out! The car is coming.
小心！車來了。

4. 表示禁止

No parking.
禁止停車。

No spitting.
禁止吐痰。

No photos.
禁止拍照。

5. 表示邀請

Come on and join us!
來加入我們吧！

Help yourself to some shrimp, please.
請別客氣自己吃蝦吧。

3. 祈使句的構成

祈使句可以有肯定式和否定式兩種形式。肯定式的祈使句就用動詞原形開始；否定式的祈使句就用 don't (或never) + 動詞原形。例如：

Be quiet, please.
請安靜。（be動詞原形開頭）

Stand up, please.
請起立。（動詞stand原形開頭）

Please be patient.
請有耐心一點。

Billy, get up at once.
比利，馬上給我起床。

Wash your hands before the meal.
吃飯前先洗手。

Don't be late.
不要遲到。

Don't move!
不要動！

Never mind.
別介意。

要注意喔！

1. 祈使句中的人名或稱呼語不是句子的主詞。例如：
Be a good boy, Tom.
湯姆，要做個好孩子喔。
（這裡的 **Tom** 不是主詞，只是稱呼。）

2. 肯定句的祈使句開頭也可以用 **do** 表示強調語氣。例如：
Do sit straight.
拜託你坐直一點。

1. 判斷看看下列句子是不是祈使句。如果是，就填「Y」，如果不是，請填「N」。

例 **Stop talking in class!** ☐ Y
　上課不要講話！

1. Look out! ☐

2. Happy New Year! ☐

3. Don't worry. ☐

4. Thank goodness! ☐

5. Get it yourself. ☐

6. Goodbye, Alice! ☐

7. Do check these answers again. ☐

8. What a terrible day! ☐

9. Quick! Turn off the gas! ☐

10. You should eat plenty of vegetables. ☐

2. 為下面的圖示選擇正確的英文提示語。

禁止游泳　　禁止釣魚　　禁止停車

1. _____　2. _____　3. _____　4. _____

A. No smoking.　B. No parking.　C. No swimming.　D. No fishing.

你做對了嗎？

	1. Y	（小心！）
	2. N	（新年快樂！）
	3. Y	（別擔心。）
	4. N	（謝天謝地！）
1.	5. Y	（你自己拿吧。）
	6. N	（再見，愛麗絲！）
	7. Y	（請再檢查一遍答案吧。）
	8. N	（真是糟糕的一天啊！）
	9. Y	（快點！把瓦斯關掉！）
	10. N	（你應該多吃蔬菜。）

2.	1. C　2. D　3. B　4. A

♥ 確實了解每一題後，再進行下一章喔！

Unit 15.
感嘆句

Unit 15. 感嘆句

① 什麼是感嘆句？

　　表示喜、怒、哀、樂等強烈感情的句子叫做感嘆句，句子結尾的地方用驚嘆號。

How clever you are!
你真聰明！

What a lovely boy he is!
他真是個可愛的男孩啊！

How interesting!
真有趣啊！

What a big pear!
好大的梨子啊！

Thank goodness!
謝天謝地！

② 感嘆句的構成方式

　　這裡介紹最基本的兩種感嘆句：由 How 和 What 開頭的感嘆句。

1. 由 How 開頭的感嘆句

　　How在感嘆句中是用來修飾形容詞或副詞的。這種句子的基本結構是：

　　How + 形容詞 / 副詞 + 主詞 + 謂語。

How wide the road is!
這條路真寬啊！　　　（How 修飾形容詞 wide）

How colorful the balloons are!
這些氣球真鮮豔！　　（How 修飾形容詞 colorful）

How fast time flies!
時間過得真快啊！　　（How 修飾副詞 fast）

How well she sings!
她唱得多好啊！　　　（How 修飾副詞 well）

　　（主詞和謂語的説明，請見p.172再複習一下吧！）

2. 由 What 開頭的感嘆句

What在感嘆句中用來修飾名詞。因為名詞有可數和不可數的區別，所以由 What 引導的感嘆句也會有兩種結構：

What + a / an + 形容詞 + 可數單數名詞 + 主詞 + 謂語

What a hardworking boy he is!
他真是一個勤奮的男孩啊！

What an interesting film it is!
這真是一部有趣的電影啊！

What + 形容詞 + 可數名詞複數（或不可數名詞）+ 主詞 + 謂語

What expensive pens these are!
這些筆真貴啊！

What pleasant weather it is!
多麼好的天氣啊！

要注意喔！

1. 有一些意思相同的感嘆句，既可以用 **How** 來開頭，也可以用 **What** 來開頭，不過句型會有一點不一樣，要注意喔！例如：

How interesting the story is!
這個故事多有趣呀！

What an interesting story it is!
這是個多麼有趣的故事！

2. 由 **How** 和 **What** 開頭的感嘆句，後面的主詞和謂語都可以省略。例如：

How sweet it is! = How sweet!
多甜美啊！

What a cool boy he is! = What a cool boy!
好酷的男孩！

1. 用how或what填空。

例 **How fast he runs!**

他跑得多快啊！

1. _____ blue the sky is!

2. _____ a beautiful song!

3. _____ deep the pond is!

4. _____ fun they are having!

5. _____ great progress Tom has made!

6. _____ high the bird is flying!

7. _____ cute the pandas are!

8. _____ a warm-hearted lady!

2. 按照題目中的要求，把下列句子改寫成感嘆句的形式。

例 **It is a long river.** （用 what 開頭）

What a long river it is!

這條河好長啊！

1. These apples are sweet. （分別用 how 和 what 開頭）

_____

_____

2. The road is crowded. （用 what 開頭）

_____

_____

3. She writes carefully.　　　（用 how 開頭）

_____

_____

4. Sharon is hard-working.　　（用 How 開頭）

_____

_____

5. Jack is a strong boy.　　　（用 what 開頭）

_____

_____

你做對了嗎？

1.

1. How（天多藍啊！）

2. What（真是好聽的歌！）

3. How（這池塘好深啊！）

4. What（他們玩得好開心啊！）

5. What（湯姆進步好多啊！）

6. How（這鳥飛得真高！）

7. How（這些熊貓好可愛啊！）

8. What（真是熱心的女士！）

解題技巧：先找到主詞，主詞前面是「形容詞」就以How開頭；主詞前面是「名詞」就以What開頭。注意：第5題，Tom是主詞，great progress 是名詞。

2.

1. How sweet these apples are!

   What sweet apples these are!（這些蘋果真甜啊！）

2. What a crowded road!（好擁擠的馬路！）

3. How carefully she writes!（她寫得好細心啊！）

4. How hard-working Sharon is!（莎倫真努力啊！）

5. What a strong boy Jack is!（傑克真是個強壯的男孩！）

♥ 確實了解每一題後，再進行下一章喔！

Unit 16.
There be 句型

There is an MP3 player. Whose is it?

那邊有個MP3，是誰的啊？

It must be Lily's. She has just gone out.

應該是莉莉的。她剛出去。

Unit 16. There be 句型

1. 讓我們來認識 There be 句型

There be 句型在英語裡表示「在某個地方有／存在什麼東西」或「在某個時間發生什麼事」，常用結構如下：

There be + 名詞 + 地點詞語 （在某個地方有／存在什麼東西）

There be + 名詞 + 時間詞語 （在某個時間發生什麼事）

2. There be 句型的用法

1. 肯定結構

There be 句型的肯定結構表示「某個地方存在著某個東西或某人」或「某個時間發生某件事」。它有兩種不同的句型結構：

1. There is + 單數可數名詞 / 不可數名詞 + 地點 / 時間詞語

There is **a bag on the chair.**
椅子上有個包包。

There is **some water in the glass.**
杯子裡有一點水。

2. There are + 複數名詞 + 地點 / 時間詞語

There are **some geese on the lake.**
湖面上有幾隻鵝。（注意：goose是單數用法，geese是複數用法）

There are **ten students in the classroom.**
教室裡有十位學生。

要注意喔！

在這種句型裡，**there** 是引導出整個句子用的詞，在句中沒有任何成分，翻譯時也不必翻出來。如果句子的主詞是一個人或一個東西，**be** 動詞要與主詞（某人或某物）的單複數對應。而如果句子的主詞是兩個或兩個以上的名詞時，**be** 動詞就要跟離它最近的那個名詞對應。例如：

There is a teacher in the office.

辦公室裡有位老師。

There is a teacher and many students in our classroom.

我們教室裡有一位老師和許多學生。

（雖然主詞是**a teacher and many students**，但是以最靠近**be**動詞的**a teacher**來判斷，所以應該用單數的**is**。）

2. 否定結構

There be 句型的否定結構是在 be 動詞的後面加「not (any)」或「no」。例如：

There are <u>no</u> chairs in the room.

There are <u>not any</u> chairs in the room.
房間裡沒有椅子。

3. 疑問結構

There be 句型變成疑問的形式時，要把 there 和 be動詞的位置互換。原單數主詞維持，複數主詞前面要加any。例如：

There is a chair in the room.
房間裡有一把椅子。（直述句）

→**Is there a chair in the room?**
房間裡有一把椅子嗎？（疑問句）

There are apple trees in the garden.
果園裡有蘋果樹。（直述句）

→**Are there any apple trees in the garden?**
果園裡有蘋果樹嗎？（疑問句加上any）

看看下面這個例子，它可以讓我們更清楚 There be 句型的三種形式有哪些分別喔！

肯定式　　**There are a lot of deer in the forest.**
　　　　　森林裡有許多隻鹿。

否定式　　**There are not any deer in the forest.**
　　　　　森林裡沒有鹿。

疑問式　　**Are there any deer in the forest?**
　　　　　森林裡有鹿嗎？

要注意喔！

There be 句型也一樣可以用於各種一般時態和完成式時態。例如：

There was a meeting yesterday.
昨天有一場會議。（過去式）

There will be a concert in the park tonight.
今晚公園裡會有一場音樂會。（未來式）

There has been no rain today.
今天沒下雨。（完成式）

1. 把正確的答案圈起來。

例 There (**is**, are) a cat on the roof.
屋頂上有一隻貓。

1. There (is, are) many girls in our family.

2. There (is, are) five sheep on the farm.

3. How many carrots (there are, are there) in the basket?

4. There (is, are) no books on the shelf.

5. There (is, was) a sports meet in our school yesterday.

6. There (is, are) a ruler and some pencils in the pencil-case.

7. (Is, Are) there something interesting in the book?

8. There are (no, not) any boats on the lake.

2. 按照題目括號裡的要求完成句子。

例 **There is some water in the basin.** （改成否定句）
盆子裡有一點水。

There isn't any water in the basin.

1. There is some rice in the bowl.
（改成一般疑問句，並做一個肯定的回答）

_____

_____

2. There is a nest in the tree.
   （改成一般疑問句，並做一個否定的回答）

   _____

   _____

3. There is a kite in the sky.
   （改成否定句）

   _____

   _____

4. There are <u>ten</u> studentss in the classroom.
   （針對劃底線的地方提出疑問）

   _____

   _____

你做對了嗎？

1.

1. are（我們家有很多女生。）

2. are（農場裡有五隻綿羊。）

3. are there（籃子裡有多少根胡蘿蔔？）

4. are（架子上沒有書。）

5. was（昨天我們學校辦了運動會。）

6. is（鉛筆盒裡有一把尺和幾支鉛筆。）
（注意：以a ruler來判斷用單數的is。）

7. Is（這本書中有什麼有趣的東西嗎？）

8. not（湖面上沒有船。）

2.

1. Is there any rice in the bowl? Yes, there is.
（碗裡有飯嗎？是的，有。）

2. Is there a nest in the tree? No, there isn't.
（樹上有鳥窩嗎？不，沒有。）

3. There isn't a kite in the sky.
（天上沒有風箏。）

4. How many students are there in the classroom?
（教室裡有多少學生？）

♥ 確實了解每一題後，再進行下一章喔！

附錄

不規則
動詞變化表

附錄 不規則動詞變化表 請特別記下來！

現在式（原形）	過去式	過去分詞	現在分詞	中文意思
am (be)	was	been	being	是
are (be)	were	been	being	是
awake	awoke	awoken	awaking	叫醒
bear	bore	born	bearing	生產、忍受
become	became	become	becoming	變得
begin	began	begun	beginning	開始
break	broke	broken	breaking	打破
bring	brought	brought	bringing	帶來
build	built	built	building	建造
buy	bought	bought	buying	買
catch	caught	caught	catching	抓住
do, does	did	done	doing	做
draw	drew	drawn	drawing	畫、拉
drink	drank	drunk	drinking	喝
drive	drove	driven	driving	開（車）
eat	ate	eaten	eating	吃
fall	fell	fallen	falling	落下
feel	felt	felt	feeling	感覺
fight	fought	fought	fighting	打架
find	found	found	finding	找到

現在式 （原形）	過去式	過去分詞	現在分詞	中文意思
fly	flew	flown	flying	飛翔
forget	forgot	forgotten	forgetting	忘記
get	got	got / gotten	getting	得到
give	gave	given	giving	給予
go	went	gone	going	去
have, has	had	had	having	有
hear	heard	heard	hearing	聽
hide	hid	hidden	hiding	躲
hold	held	held	holding	握住、舉行
hurt	hurt	hurt	hurting	傷害
is (be)	was	been	being	是
keep	kept	kept	keeping	保持
know	knew	known	knowing	知道
learn	learned / learnt	learned / learnt	learning	學習
leave	left	left	leaving	離開
lend	lent	lent	lending	借
lie	lay	lain	lying	躺
lose	lost	lost	losing	弄丟
make	made	made	making	做
meet	met	met	meeting	遇見
mistake	mistook	mistaken	mistaking	誤會
pay	paid	paid	paying	付錢

現在式 （原形）	過去式	過去分詞	現在分詞	中文意思
ride	rode	ridden	riding	騎乘
ring	rang	rung	ringing	響
rise	rose	risen	rising	升起
run	ran	run	running	跑
say	said	said	saying	說
see	saw	seen	seeing	看
sell	sold	sold	selling	賣
send	sent	sent	sending	送出
shake	shook	shaken	shaking	搖晃
shoot	shot	shot	shooting	射
sing	sang	sung	singing	唱歌
sit	sat	sat	sitting	坐
sleep	slept	slept	sleeping	睡覺
speak	spoke	spoken	speaking	說
spend	spent	spent	spending	花（錢）
stand	stood	stood	standing	站
strike	struck	struck	striking	打擊
swim	swam	swum	swimming	游泳
take	took	taken	taking	拿取
teach	taught	taught	teaching	教
tell	told	told	telling	告訴
think	thought	thought	thinking	想

現在式 （原形）	過去式	過去分詞	現在分詞	中文意思
understand	understood	understood	understanding	了解
wear	wore	worn	wearing	穿
win	won	won	winning	贏
write	wrote	written	writing	寫

動詞原形、過去式、過去分詞三者相同的動詞變化：

現在式 （原形）	過去式	過去分詞	現在分詞	中文意思
cut	cut	cut	cutting	切
hit	hit	hit	hitting	打
let	let	let	letting	讓
put	put	put	putting	放
read	read	read	reading	讀書
set	set	set	setting	設置

原來如此 系列 E069

五億人重新開始的第一本**英文文法書**

重新開始和英文做朋友，沒有那麼難！

作　　者	薄冰
顧　　問	曾文旭
總 編 輯	王毓芳
編輯統籌	耿文國
主　　編	林侑音
執行編輯	張辰安
美術編輯	吳靜宜、王桂芳
封面設計	阿作
法律顧問	北辰著作權事務所　蕭雄淋律師、嚴裕欽律師

印　　製	世和印製企業有限公司
初　　版	2013年1月
出　　版	捷徑文化出版事業有限公司
電　　話	（02）6636-8398
傳　　真	（02）6636-8397
地　　址	106 台北市大安區忠孝東路四段218-7號7樓

定　　價	新台幣299元／港幣100元
產品內容	1書

總 經 銷	采舍國際有限公司
地　　址	235 新北市中和區中山路二段366巷10號3樓
電　　話	（02）8245-8786
傳　　真	（02）8245-8718

港澳地區總經銷	和平圖書有限公司
地　　址	香港柴灣嘉業街12號百樂門大廈17樓
電　　話	（852）2804-6687
傳　　真	（852）2804-6409

本書原由開明出版社以書名《薄冰小學英語語法》首次出版。此中文繁體字版由開明出版社授權捷徑文化出版事業有限公司在臺灣、香港和澳門地區獨家出版發行。僅供上述地區銷售。

捷徑 Book站

即日起只要到臉書「捷徑Book站」粉絲團按讚，並私訊告訴我們你買了捷徑哪本書、從哪本書得知此活動，並留下聯絡方式，即可任選一本捷徑出版的書，我們將免費贈送給您！每年您的生日當月更會收到我們一份驚喜小禮物喔！

http://www.facebook.com/royalroadbooks
讀者來函：royalroadbooks@gmail.com

國家圖書館出版品預行編目資料

五億人重新開始的第一本英文文法書 / 薄冰著.
-- 初版. -- 臺北市：捷徑文化, 2013.01
　面；　公分(原來如此：E069)
ISBN 978-986-6010-51-4(平裝)

1. 英語　2. 語法

805.16　　　　　　　　　　　　101025264

文法是英文學習不可或缺的一環，
有了文法觀念才能**串連單字**、**片語**，進而**組成句子**，
現在，跟著薄冰老師
用最淺顯、清楚、易懂的方式和大量例句學英文文法
想要從頭開始，就選：
五億人重新開始的第一本英文文法書！

捷徑文化
Royal Road Publishing Group